LOVE

love

THE KEATYN CHRONICLES: BOOK 12

JILLIAN DODD

Editor: Jovana Shirley, Unforeseen Editing, www.unforeseenediting.com

Jillian Dodd Inc.
N. Redington Beach, FL

EVEN KEATS SPEAKS OF CHAOS.
There is nothing stable in the world;
uproar's your only music.

Books by Jillian Dodd

The Keatyn Chronicles
USA TODAY bestselling young adult contemporary romance set in an East Coast boarding school.
Stalk Me
Kiss Me
Date Me
Love Me
Adore Me
Hate Me
Get Me
Fame
Power
Money
Sex
Love

Keatyn Unscripted
Aiden

That Boy Series
Small-town contemporary romance series about falling in love with the boy next door.
That Boy
That Wedding
That Baby
That Divorce

The Love Series
Contemporary, standalone romances following the very sexy Crawford family.
Vegas Love
Broken Love
Fake Love

Spy Girl Series
Young adult romance series about a young spy who just might save the world.
The Prince
The Eagle
The Society
The Valiant

Jillian Dodd and Kenzie Harp
Young adult travel romance.
Girl off the Grid

TUESDAY, OCTOBER 28TH
KEATYN & AIDEN'S HOME - CHELSEA

Riley

"HAPPY BIRTHDAY!" DALLAS says as I sit down at the kitchen table. "How are you feeling?"

"Pretty good. I didn't drink much last night. The bachelor party did me in."

He laughs. "And I'm the opposite. I was too busy videoing the bachelor party to drink much. Last night was another story."

"Yeah, when you started singing"—I smirk—"I knew it was time to cut you off."

"But you didn't."

"Ha! You're right about that. You deserved it!"

Keatyn wanders into the room, wrapped up in a long cashmere robe. Her hair is piled on top of her head, and she has dark circles under her eyes.

"Are you feeling okay?" I ask.

"Yeah," she says, putting on a fake smile. Although she's a good actress, I've known her long enough now that she can't fool me. "I'm fine. Just been up late the past few nights, and it's catching up to me."

"You're supposed to be relaxing on your honeymoon," I reply, feeling bad. "I hope our being here hasn't totally ruined it."

1

"Of course it hasn't, Riley! I would have flown here from wherever we were to be at Knox and Katie's wedding. And it has been so fun, having you all here to break in the new house. I do have a bit of a cold though. Probably from switching climates."

My phone buzzes, causing me to look down. "Shit."

"What's wrong?"

I set my phone down in frustration. "I thought it might be Shelby. I've texted her a few times since Sunday when I canceled our dinner plans, and still, no word. At first, I thought she was just mad that I went out of town without telling her why—or inviting her with—but now, I'm starting to get a little worried."

"Call the hotel," Dallas offers. "Have them check on her."

"That's a good idea." I make the call.

"I'm sorry, Mr. Johnson," the hotel manager says. "Miss Benson has not been in her room in a few days—since Sunday, I believe."

"Is her stuff all still there?"

"Yes, sir."

"Is she okay?"

"I believe so."

"Do you know where she is?"

"I really am not at liberty to discuss our guest's personal life," he states.

"I'm paying for her room. I think you are well aware of that."

"Uh, yes, sir."

"She's pregnant with my child. I would like to know where she is or any information you might have before I contact the police."

"Oh, sir, that isn't necessary," he backtracks. "I can assure you that she is on a planned trip."

"Do you know where to?"

"She did not leave word as to her destination, but it's my understanding that she will be returning."

"Thank you," I say, hanging up, frustrated.

"I take it, he didn't tell you anything?" Dallas asks.

"Nothing other than she is on a planned trip. Where would she go?"

"I don't know. Somewhere with a friend? To see family?" Keatyn offers.

"Shit. When she was mad at me about Ariela, she threatened to move back home with her mother. She told me that she'd raise the baby without me. She can't do that, can she?"

"Calm down, Riley," Dallas says as Keatyn takes a three-tiered confetti birthday cake out of the refrigerator, sets it in front of me, and starts adding a whole freaking lot of candles to it. "I'm sure she and the baby are fine. The legal answer to your question is, right now, she can do whatever she wants. Once the baby is born, you'll have more rights, and we'll make sure you do."

"I'm still worried about her. She left home when she was young, but she did mention that her mom had gotten her life back together—whatever that means."

"You care about her, don't you?" Keatyn asks, handing a lighter to Dallas. "Here, light these. You've always been better at it than me."

Dallas grins.

"Yeah, I guess I do care about her," I reply. "The ultrasound photo kinda did me in."

"Happy birthday, Riley!" Keatyn yells out, interrupting the conversation and giving me a hug. "Wow, twenty-nine. You're practically over the hill!"

"No, that will be your husband in another month," I sass. "He's turning the big three-oh."

"I don't think he cares. He's excited about it. I remember when I used to think thirty was practically ancient!"

"Me, too. And, yet, here we are."

"Speak for yourself." She laughs. "I still have a year and a half before I turn thirty! And, thankfully, I will hit my goal of having my first child before that milestone. In fact, if all goes well, I'll triple it."

Once the candles are all glowing, lighting up the room like a damn spotlight, she and Dallas start singing.

When they are finished, Keatyn says, "Make a wish, Riley!"

I stare into the flames and know exactly what I want. *Ariela.* I close my eyes. *I want to stop blaming her. I want to stop being mad at her for the past. I want to stop fucking Shelby. I want Ariela to get a divorce and marry me, and I'll spend a lifetime making up for the ten years we lost—*

"You'd better hurry up and make a wish before we burn down the new house," Dallas teases.

I don't open my eyes. I hold the wish in my head and blow out the candles.

While Keatyn takes the candles off and cuts huge wedges for each of us, I tell her and Dallas something that has been on my mind. "I've been thinking about buying that house in Sonoma as a birthday present to myself."

"Riley, you know I would be excited to have you close, and you have to do what's right for you, but tell me why you want to buy it."

I shrug. "It feels like the kind of place where I could grow old with someone."

"And which someone do you want to grow old with?" she asks.

"The other day, I did that thing Grandpa Douglas told you about—how, when you can't decide what to do—"

"You resorted to a coin flip?" Dallas asks, furrowing his brows.

I lower my head in shame and nod.

Keatyn rubs the top of my hand, and it makes me feel stronger. She can do that. Sometimes, Dallas gives me a hard time, but Keatyn is the opposite. I guess maybe she's been through enough that she's more understanding. Less demanding. More like she'd help guide me down the right path. And I wish she would. I wish someone would just decide for me. Someone who knows what my right path is. If I take the risk I want more than anything to take, it's going to be difficult. It's going to test me. And, even though Ariela is what I wished for, what I want, I'm afraid I'm not up for the challenge.

"What did you learn, Riley?" she asks gently.

"The first person I thought of was Ariela. She's who I want more than anything. She's who I've dreamed of spending my life with. And, even though she has changed over the last ten years, she's still my girl."

"So then, you know. It's Ariela."

"At your wedding, I would have answered that question with a yes. We talked, and everything she said made me feel so much better. She told me that she was weak when she broke up with me. That she was young and scared and foolish then, but that she's not anymore. She told me she wants to be with me and that she wasn't afraid to tell me that she still loves me."

"Aw, Riley," Keatyn says, visibly melting and then shoving a big bite of cake in her mouth. There's nothing that gets to her like a good love story.

"Oh, it gets better." I grin, egging her on. "I asked her what she wanted from our relationship, going forward."

"Is this going to get all mushy?" Dallas teases. "If so, I might have to go throw up."

"Shut up, Dallas!" Keatyn says, swatting his arm. "You have no room to talk, *pookie bear.*"

Dallas shrugs my comment off with a laugh.

"Keep going, Riley," Keatyn encourages.

"The night of your wedding was when we were supposed to decide if we wanted to go forward—like, if we wanted to date. So, I asked her what she wanted. At first, she said that she just wants me. Then she told me that wasn't true. That what she wants is to marry me, have babies with me, and love me until I'm old and gray."

"Ohmigod, that's so sweet, Riley. How did it make you feel? Can you do that? Can you let go of the hurt and be happy with her?"

"Yes, I can, but—"

"There's not supposed to be a *but*, Riley," she chastises.

"There is when the *butt* is attached to someone who looks like Shelby." Dallas lets out a laugh. He's teasing but not.

"Right. If Shelby wasn't in the picture, I'd be with Ariela right now. When I flipped the coin, I thought of Ariela, but I also thought of the ultrasound photo and Shelby."

Dallas rolls his eyes while Keatyn presses her finger into her brow—something she does when she's feeling stressed. I grab her hand and pull it away.

"Aiden has given me strict orders not to stress you. Where is he anyway?"

"He had a meeting this morning."

"Wine stuff?"

"Sort of. I want to tell you about it, but we need to finish this conversation first. So, when you flipped the coin, you saw them both."

"Dude," Dallas says, leaning back in his chair, "you're giving me emotional whiplash."

"That's exactly how I've been feeling and why this has been so difficult. I love Ariela, but I have to think about Shelby and the baby."

"Riley, you don't even know for sure if it's yours," Dallas stresses.

"I believe it is. I didn't want a baby. I certainly didn't want one with Shelby. But I've grown to care for her. And the baby."

"But can you picture yourself marrying her and living happily ever after?" Keatyn challenges.

I open my mouth to speak, but Dallas raises his hand. "Wait. Before you answer that question, I want you to consider a few points."

"Okay," I say with a smirk. "What have you got, counselor?"

"You told me that Ariela won't sleep with you again until you are in a monogamous relationship. Why do you think that is?"

"Because she loves me, and she's crazy jealous of Shelby," I answer.

"Correct. Now, what does it say about Shelby that she's willing to share you?"

"She doesn't love me the way Ariela does," I state, already knowing what he's thinking.

"So, who should you choose?" he asks.

"Ariela."

"And who *will* you choose?"

"Before I answer that, I have a few questions for you two," I say. "Ariela handled dealing with Shelby very poorly. Does that mean they will never get along?"

"No, it doesn't," Keatyn says. "It's going to take some time for Ariela and Shelby to establish a relationship. It's a sort of messed up situation, but that doesn't mean it can't work. The reason it went poorly the first time is because you were sleeping with them both. That created competition. Until you decide who you want and stick to it, they won't get along." She stops and considers things for a moment. "Honestly, once you choose, you know what will happen."

"Yes, if I choose Shelby and the baby, I will lose Ariela completely."

"And how does that make you feel?" Dallas asks.

"It wrecks me," I say. "I know you are trying to help me figure it out, but I don't think it's necessary. The coin toss did actually clarify things for me."

"But you said you saw them both, Riley." Keatyn sighs. "You can't have them both."

"Yes, I can. I want to marry Ariela as soon as she gets a divorce. I want to buy the Sonoma house, raise a family, and love her forever. But I also want my child in my life—"

Dallas stops me with a raise of his eyebrow.

"*If* it's mine, Shelby will be a part of my life as well. When the coin flipped, I saw the ultrasound photo, not Shelby herself. I won't deny that I have feelings for Shelby, but they are feelings I wouldn't have for her if she wasn't pregnant."

I shove a big bite of cake in my mouth as my phone buzzes again. This time, it's my brother.

"Hang on," I say, answering. "Need to swallow."

"That's what she said," Dawson teases.

"I'm eating birthday cake. Get your mind out of the gutter."

"And that's why I'm calling," he says. "To wish you a happy birthday."

"Thanks."

"Mom says this coming weekend is going to be one big celebration, including my little brother's last birthday of his twenties. Dad says we will be drinking Irish whiskey."

"Oh, gosh, no," I beg. "Anything but that. How about some nice tequila?"

"Anything you want. Hey, um, I think you should bring the ultrasound photo with you, show it to Mom and Dad. You need to tell them."

"I was kind of waiting to see if it was mine or not first. Please don't mention it to them."

"Mom gets a Google alert every time your name is mentioned. She saw the baby-mama-drama post."

"Well, shit," I say. "I guess I'll have to come clean about it then. See you in a few days."

I hang up just as Keatyn finishes her cake. Her skin is starting to brighten. Maybe she just needed some food.

But then she covers her mouth with her hand. "Oh, crap," she says, rushing off.

Dallas and I cringe when we hear her puking up the cake.

He sets his fork down. "I think I'm done now."

I laugh, then figure, *Screw it*, and keep eating my cake the entire time she's puking. It's my fucking birthday after all.

BEFORE KEATYN GETS back from the bathroom, her chef, Marvel, comes into the room. When he walks into a kitchen anywhere in the world, he takes command of the space.

"I'm told your customary birthday meal is chicken and waffles. I have taken the liberty of preparing the fried chicken but wanted to wait until you had awoken before cooking the waffles. I have to say, this is a very odd combination."

"You've never had chicken and waffles?" Dallas asks. "Marvel, you are in for a treat."

Marvel sticks his nose up in the air, like the thought is beneath him, and gets to work, heating up a large waffle iron and then pouring an already prepped batter into it. Soon, the room is filled with a wonderful sweet scent.

"Oh, that smells good," Keatyn says, returning.

"You feel okay?" I ask.

"Yeah, I'm fine. Being pregnant is kind of weird. The nausea comes on suddenly, but for the most part, it's over just as quickly. Like, I'm ready to eat some breakfast now."

"Thank you for making my favorite," I say gratefully, locking eyes with her.

She's been my best friend for so long, and she never forgets stuff like this.

I get up to give her a squeeze. "Thank you."

"You're welcome, Riley. You know I love you."

"Better not let your new husband hear that," Aiden teases as he comes into the room. He's dressed up. Full suit, tie, and wing tips.

"You look hot as fuck," Keatyn says, letting out a whistle and fanning her face. "What is it about a man in a suit?"

I stare at her in shock. She doesn't usually speak so vulgar. Maybe it's the pregnancy talking.

"Why are you all dressed up so early in the morning?" Dallas asks.

Aiden laughs and glances at his watch. "It's almost noon. Speaking of that, do I smell Riley's usual birthday meal? Chicken and waffles?"

"You know it," Dallas says. "Marvel isn't so sure about the combination though."

"So, where were you?" I ask Aiden. "Keatyn said something about a business meeting. Moon Wish stuff?"

"No, actually, there's a reason we bought a home in London. Keatyn and I are going to be here more often. And, with the babies coming, I can't imagine staying in hotels."

"Is this the wine-bar thing you mentioned?" Dallas asks.

I swear, he always knows everything that's going on with everyone.

"Yeah, I met with the engineer and the owner of the construction company we've chosen to restore the hotel. If all goes well, we'll be open in four months. The structure is in surprisingly good shape, so that was great news. And we can get it going before the babies are born."

"Wait," I say. "You're opening a hotel?"

"No, it's sort of a weird concept. A restaurant combined with a wine-tasting room and retail space. Like what we have at the vineyard. I bought an old hotel building that we've nearly stripped down to the studs."

"It's going to be so cool," Keatyn interjects. "It's got a lot of character that will be combined with an industrial look to give it a laid-back vibe. And the best part is, it's got three floors upstairs that he's turning into a private club."

"Well, you know who your first members will be," I say. "Congrats, Aiden."

"Thanks, man," he says, grinning. "And happy birthday."

"It does mean, however," Keatyn adds gently, "that we might not be in Sonoma *quite* as much as we originally planned, but I hope that doesn't discourage you from buying that house, Riley. Captive's new studios are definitely still a go."

BAM'S YACHT – PACIFIC OCEAN
Shelby

WHEN JUAN DOESN'T come back from wherever he went, I move to a chaise lounge, figuring I'm bound to get kicked off the yacht before lunch.

Oh well, might as well enjoy the luxury while it lasts.

I slip off my cover-up, revealing a tasteful one-piece, and position myself to soak up some sun on this beautiful day. The breeze is a little chilly, but the sun warms me. I close my eyes and try to imagine what it would be like to be married to a man like Juan Fabio Martinez.

Of course, after we slept together, I was feeling obsessed and searched him on the Internet. There were photos of him with numerous women throughout the years. He was married at one point to a woman named Vanessa, but I'd bet money that he wasn't faithful to her. It doesn't matter that he is fabulously wealthy and a famous polo player; the man has the kind of charisma money can't buy. The kind of man who makes women drop their panties. Those kind of men can be found in every social class. I should know. I have probably fallen for them all.

I hear a ruckus and open my eyes. Juan is standing above me. And he's in a tuxedo.

"I think I might be a tad underdressed," I tease. "You look quite handsome."

His eyes feast on my body before he replies, "And you look like a temptress."

"I'm tempting you?" I chuckle, glancing down at myself. "This is my most conservative swimsuit."

"Well, I have seen you naked, so I am most pleasantly aware of what is underneath." He smiles. "I have a proposition for you."

"What kind of proposition?" I ask, expecting it to be something of a sexual nature. And I'm all for that. Hell, I'm just thrilled he's still here, and I haven't gotten kicked off the boat yet.

He pulls a small box out of his jacket pocket and gets down on one knee.

Wait, did he say proposition or proposal?

"I, Juan Fabio Martinez, am asking for your hand in marriage. I will raise your child as my own, and we will have many more heirs. Not only can I give you a life of luxury, but I also promise to treat you like royalty because that is exactly how you deserve to be treated. After hearing what you said about gifts with meaning, before I present you with this ring of my commitment, I feel the desire to explain."

When he hesitates, I realize that I'm shaking.

Did I fall asleep? Am I dreaming this?

"My mother gave me this ring to present to the woman I would marry," he continues. "It was not chosen with you in mind, but I believe in the deepest recesses of my heart that you were whom she had in mind when she gave it to me. Will you marry me, Shelby?"

I start to reply, but just then he opens the box to reveal a gem so big, it belongs in a museum.

"I, uh," I stutter.

"It's all right," he says. "I understand. It is a shock. We have known each other for a very short time, but during that time together, you've made me feel different, more so than any woman has before you. My mother tells me that I am like my father—raging hormones, too many for one woman—but she is wrong. You are the only woman I will ever need. May I put this ring on your finger?"

I burst out in a happy, maniacal-sounding laugh. "Yes!" I scream.

When he slides it on my finger, we both discover that it fits.

"See? A perfect fit. Further proof that it was made just for you."

I throw my arms around his neck and kiss him. That leads to me straddling him on the chaise and doing him right there on the deck—for all the world, or any passing boats, to see.

Whatever.

Who fucking cares?

I'm going to marry a gazillionaire, and I'm actually in love with him.

AFTER OUR CELEBRATORY fuck, I ask Juan about the ring—because, holy shit, this ring—"Is this, like, a sapphire or a blue topaz?"

"No, my darling," he says with a laugh. "It is a *very* rare blue diamond. A gift to my mother from my father. She never took the time to have it set until she decided to give it to me. It is a modest twelve carats, but because of the rarity of the stone, it is worth much more than a colorless diamond of the same size."

"I have no idea what either would be worth."

"Well, if it were a flawless colorless diamond, it would be worth five million. The ring that so perfectly fits your finger is worth around twenty-five."

"Million?" I gasp. "Oh, Juan, I can't wear this. It's too much. Someone will try to steal it or something." I slip it off my finger and shove it toward him. "Here, take it. If you're serious about marrying me, that's great. But I don't even need a ring. Really."

Juan just smiles at me. "You know, my friends all call me Bam."

"Bam sounds like a boy's name."

His smile becomes wider. "You're right. I adore that you call me by

12

my given name. My mother will love you."

"Do you think?"

"Yes, but you mustn't offend her by not wearing the ring."

"So, I only have to wear it when we are with her?"

He takes my hand and slides it back on my finger. God, it's freaking beautiful.

"You must wear it always. And you must travel to Italy with me today. There is to be a ball celebrating the Dia de los Muertos, the Day of the Dead. It is a holiday not typically celebrated in my home country, but it is an important part of my mother's heritage, so she always throws a party. Because she's lived all over the world, it's sort of a mash-up of traditions, but it's fun. A masked ball on the thirty-first to celebrate Halloween. At just after midnight, there is a great feast to celebrate All Saints' Day. The party goes on all night, ending with a festive parade mid-afternoon on the castle grounds."

"I thought your parents lived in Argentina."

"That's where my father is from, where I was born, and where many of our business interests are, but they have many homes and travel often." He lowers his head. "Well, they used to. Now, my father is ill."

"But they are still having the party? Isn't that sort of morbid?"

"It celebrates both the living and the dead. Since my father is still among the living, he will celebrate with us. And he will be thrilled to meet you and learn of our engagement and, eventually, of your pregnancy." He pauses. "It will mean, however, that you will have to lie about the baby's paternity. Are you willing to do that?"

"You will be the only father the baby ever knows," I answer sincerely.

"You have no idea how overjoyed my parents will be."

"Tell me about the castle. Is it haunted? Drafty?"

"While it is quite old, it's been painstakingly renovated over the last fifteen years, and it is quite luxurious. No drafty parts. It has maybe thirty bedrooms, about forty thousand square feet. Want to know the best part about it?"

"Yes!" I can only imagine how amazing it must be.

"It has a Roman chapel on the grounds, and the gardens can accommodate over three hundred guests. I want you to plan your dream wedding. No expense shall be spared. But I would like you to consider it as a possible venue. It would make me very happy."

"That's where we'll do it then. My new goal in life is to make you happy. Speaking of that, what would you think of retiring to your bedroom?"

"I think it sounds like you're going to make me happy very quickly."

"Not too quickly, I hope," I flirt.

Fucking A. What a day!

WEDNESDAY, OCTOBER 29TH
ASHER VINEYARDS – SONOMA COUNTY
Ariela

"SOMEONE IS HERE to see you," Kyle says.

"Who?" I ask, swiveling my chair around.

Kyle walks over to the arched window that overlooks the tasting room and points down. "Your mother."

"My mother? Why didn't she tell me she was coming?"

"Do you want the condensed version?" he asks with a smirk. "Look, I know we're crazy busy, and this isn't the best time, but it's your mom. And it's quite possible that, when she called to talk to you the other day and you told me to tell her that you would call her back because you were busy—that she called back. And we may have had a very long and heartfelt conversation. One that I was sucked into, much in the same way I had been when I met you at the coffee shop that day. Hell, all I wanted to do was get laid. Now, look at me." He sweeps his arms out at the gorgeous office that he's managed to put together for me. "First, I play shrink to you and tell you to go to California to find Riley. I somehow end up here. Now, I'm paying it forward. I suggested that your mom come to Cali. And I maybe didn't tell you because I didn't want you to tell her no."

I smile at Kyle, give him a quick peck on the cheek, and rush toward the stairs.

"Let's see. I got a kiss on the cheek for bringing your mom. What do I have to do to get laid? That's what I want to know."

I turn around and stick my tongue out at him. "You'd better watch it, or I'll tell Keatyn all about your texts to her little sister."

"We're just friends."

"Uh-huh," I sass back as I run down the stairs.

"Mom! What are you doing here?" I say, throwing my arms around her in a surprisingly affectionate gesture.

If she's startled by my hug, she doesn't show it. She simply hugs me tighter. And, in that instant, I know, whatever happens going forward, I can get through it because she's finally on my side.

"Your lovely assistant said that I should come see where you work," she states. "He really does have a sexy phone voice. I couldn't wait to meet him in person." She gives me a wink. "And he did not disappoint. I suspect that having an assistant who looks like that makes coming to work every day quite enjoyable." She tilts her head. "Damn. I just realized that's probably what our husbands thought about their assistants. Is Kyle single? Are you having a fling with him?"

"Mom." I take a deep breath, slowing her down, and try to figure out how to answer the question.

Kyle sneaks up and wraps his arm around my mother's shoulders. "Sadly, boss lady and I are not flinging as of yet. She's all hung up on that Riley guy."

"Oh, how I wish I were younger," my mother flirts.

"Um, so you just flew here without telling me?" I ask.

She glances at a tour group that has just entered the tasting room. "Why don't we go outside, dear?"

I lead her outside to a bench placed in the shade of an olive tree. "I'm so excited you're here."

My mother actually blushes. "I was afraid you might not want me here. That's why I didn't let you know in advance."

"After what you said to Dad?"

She absentmindedly straightens her shirt, so it won't wrinkle as she sits. "I'm worried about your father," she says. "Do you think I was too hard on him?"

"I think you were too easy on him in the past, and it all came out at once. I think what you did was awesome."

"It's hard though when you love someone. I loved your father despite his faults."

"By faults, you mean, his infidelity?"

"Yes. And, in some ways, what I did was unfaithful as well."

"Dad and his accountant knew exactly what they were doing when they transferred assets to you. They just didn't think you understood the significance of it."

"I lied to your father. I hadn't been looking the other way until I had control of his company. I was being vengeful. I put up with his cheating because I didn't think I had any other options, and I was worried about what people would think of me.

"I'm very sorry for what I said to you at the florist. Your boldness and willingness to leave the man you loved because he was a lying bastard affected me. I gave you horrible advice. Advice I wish I had never followed myself.

"When I went home, I looked in the mirror and saw someone who was horribly unhappy with her life but didn't have the balls to do something about it. I thought about how freeing it would be to not have to carry the weight of an unhappy marriage on my shoulders. And that's when I remembered the house was in my name, the company was almost mine, and I had your father by the short hairs."

"And how do you feel now?"

"Exhilarated. Like a new woman. Young and free."

"But you're still worried about Dad?"

She rolls her eyes. "Yes, the bastard is a wreck. I can sort of see why he took a lover now. We married when we were young, and he'd yet to experience the real world. I took over where his mother had left off and became his caretaker. Funny, his playthings don't seem to be stepping in to make sure his clothes are clean, his place is spotless, or if there is food in his pantry. And it seems to perplex him. Yesterday, we met with the mediator. We're trying to settle the financial details before seeing a judge."

"And he looked bad?"

"Yes, his suit looked like he'd slept in it. He's gained weight because he's probably been drinking more, eating out, and not meeting with his trainer. I've always watched his salt and caloric intake because he's borderline pre-diabetic. Do you think I am being too hard on him?"

"I think you have a lot of pent-up anger toward him. But I'm certainly no relationship expert. I have no idea what I'm doing. Quite frankly, the best advice I've gotten recently was that I should focus on loving myself. That, if I do, I'll be a good partner. I won't need a man in my life to make me happy but will have him in it because he enhances my life. Because I have fun with him."

"Is Riley going to be that man?"

"I'm not sure, Mom. Things are complicated."

She laughs. "They always are, dear." She looks around. "Think we can get a bottle of wine in this place?"

I laugh, too. "Yeah, I think we can."

We go back into the tasting room and grab a new rose vintage, and I introduce her to Keatyn's grandmother, Maggie, and one of the sommeliers, Chad.

"Are you hungry?" Grandma Douglas asks us.

"I actually am a little. Is there a restaurant nearby?" my mother asks.

"I think we can rustle you up a snack. Ariela, why don't you show your mother the grounds? And I'll have a late lunch set up on the terrace of your guesthouse in about thirty minutes."

My mother gives Maggie a hug on the way out, causing us to share a startled look because my mother has never been a hugger. "It's so good to see you again, Maggie," she says. "Hopefully, I'll be seeing a lot more of you."

"Um, are you planning to stay for a while?" I ask delicately as I lead my mother outside and to a golf cart.

We get in, and I drive us up the hill toward Keatyn and Aiden's estate.

"It's really beautiful here," she says, avoiding the question. "The hills, the valleys, the rows of grapes. It's all so lush and green."

"Wait until we get up to the top. You can see the ocean in the distance," I tell her.

"I can see why you don't want to come home."

"The view isn't why I'm not coming home, Mom. There are pretty places to live everywhere. It's funny. I came out here to find Riley and ended up finding myself.

"With Collin, I had become a shell. I had given up on my dreams because he didn't support them.

"Ever since I started in the event-planning business, from my very first internship, I've been hooked. I've dreamed of having my own company. Calling the shots. Doing events the way I want to. Fewer events, more attention to details. Perfectly executed details are what I do best.

"I had no idea when I came here on a whim that Keatyn would ask me to do her wedding. I had no idea of the demand it would create. But I'm now officially living my dream.

"Would I like Riley in my life? Yes. I love him. Never stopped. But he would only enhance my already wonderful life. He wouldn't be the reason for my existence, which is a much more empowering and wonderful way to love."

"That's what I want," she says, tears filling her eyes. "Believe it or not, I've considered taking your father back. That's the real reason I hopped on a plane here. I'm afraid I'll do it, that I'll get sucked back into our old ways, old habits, old feelings. I need to find myself and reignite my passions."

"Is there anything you ever dreamed about doing?"

She gazes into the distance. After a few seconds, she whispers, "Flowers. I've planned so many charity events over the years, and flowers are the reason I've kept doing them. You know, before I met your father, I worked in a floral shop. The owner got really sick, and I had to do a funeral by myself once. The family sent me a thank-you note, complimenting me on the design. The owner wanted me to go to floral design school."

"Maybe you should do that now." I grin at her. "Or maybe you could help me. I'm actually looking for a liaison to work with florists. To make sure their designs end up being exactly what we envision for our clients."

"You'd hire me?"

"Of course I would. You are more anal than I am, yet you're still quite creative."

"I'd have to move here."

"Yes. You'd also be doing a fair amount of travel. Our clients want us to come to them, wherever they happen to be in the world."

"Do you think we could work together?" she asks.

I smile at her. "I think so. As long as you remember who the boss is."

"Kyle?" she replies with a grin.

"Exactly."

WE'RE SITTING ON the terrace, just finishing up lunch, when my cell rings.

I glance at it. "Collin."

"Are you going to answer?"

I sigh. "I probably should. Do you mind?"

"Of course not. I think I'll get up and stretch my legs. Maybe walk down to the tasting room."

"Okay, I'll meet you there in a few." I answer the phone, "This is Ariela."

"And this is your husband," Collin replies.

"Hey, Collin. What's up?" I say cheerfully, refusing to let him to spoil my day.

"*What's up?* Really, Ariela? Have you turned into some stoner surfer out there? What has happened to your vocabulary?"

"I'm in a good mood, Collin, and I'm busy. What is the reason for your call?"

"I'm your husband. I don't need a reason."

"Well, if there isn't a reason for your call, I'll just say that it has been utterly delightful to hear your voice, but I must go."

"Fine. We need to discuss the divorce."

"What about it?"

"I don't want it."

"Why not? I'm being more than fair. My attorney even thinks I'm being stupid in all that I'm giving you."

"It doesn't matter what you give me. I want you to come home. I'll fix everything. I'll be the man you want me to be. I swear it."

"What's wrong, Collin?" I ask, knowing that's not the real reason for his call.

He sighs. "I guess I didn't realize all you do for me. I don't even know which cleaners you went to. I must have gone to the wrong one. They completely ruined two of my dress shirts and lost the pants to one of my suits."

"It's on the outside of the bag, Collin."

"The pants?"

"No, the name of the cleaners I used, along with their address. Sounds like you need to hire a housekeeper. Someone who can do all those meaningless tasks you expected me to make my life's work and still feel fulfilled."

"I get it, okay? I've been a bad husband." He lets out an exasperated sigh. "I thought we were a team. Whatever. The reason for my call is that my attorney just informed me that we have a court date. It's soon. And I'm freaking out a little. We used to be friends, Ariela. I have no one to talk to."

I nearly suggest he talk to his lover, but I take a deep breath. I just have to get through this. Get on with my life.

"I'm happy to talk to you about it, Collin," I lie. The last thing I want to do is talk to him about it. I want to scream and yell at him for cheating on me, but at the same time, I feel like discovering the truth was a gift. He had been pressuring me to have children. To quit my job.

If I had done those things and then found out—I can't even imagine. When I found out about his infidelity, it was a horrible shock. I was pissed. Hurt. But, now, I realize that finding out was the best thing to happen to me.

"I screwed up," he says. "I know that. But it was a mistake."

"Sleeping with your secretary for months was a mistake? All the other girls, they were mistakes, too?"

"I just needed it for me. I know that probably doesn't make sense—"

"Actually, it makes perfect sense. And it's why I tried to get you to go to counseling in the past. It's exactly why *you* need this divorce. You went to other women because you were seeking attention. Your ego masks your lack of self-confidence. Your issues need to be addressed, Collin. And, if you don't work on them, they will destroy your life, just like they destroyed our marriage. I loved you. I wish you the best. But we are most definitely getting a divorce. The question is, do you want to drag the process out or get on with your life?"

"Our court date is in thirty days. Not much time for dragging. Guess I'll see you then."

"I guess you will."

I hang up my phone and circle the date in red on my calendar. If all goes well, I'll be a free woman very soon.

BAM'S CASTLE – TURIN, ITALY

Shelby

WE ARRIVE IN Turin, Italy, late in the afternoon. My breath is quickly taken away by the view. The majestic Alps rise to the northwest of the city, the village is red-roofed, and stately buildings line the boulevards.

Juan points upward to an ancient stone castle surrounded by a wall. "There it is. What do you think?"

"It looks a little drafty," I tease, causing him to shut me up with a kiss.

"The wall surrounding the castle was built between the ninth and fourteenth century, and the castle was once owned by King Arduino, the Bishop of Ivrea, and even the Holy Roman Emperor, Otto the first."

"You've seen one castle, you've seen them all, I suspect."

He pulls me close and tickles my sides, causing me to screech.

"Juan! Behave!"

"Oh, but you don't like it when I behave," he teases back.

"True, but I'm nervous."

"Don't be. My mother will adore you if you follow a few simple rules. Do not use the Lord's name in vain, do not curse—that one is particularly difficult for me—and no fake laughing. She says that is the guise of the devil. You are a beautiful woman, and I have chosen you as my bride. In my family, a wife is placed above all others, to be respected."

"Except you cheated on your first wife?" I ask, wondering if it's all bullshit.

"Yes."

"So, you don't follow your family's rules, in other words. Does your father?"

He laughs. "My father has had numerous dalliances over the years."

"And, in your family, that is not considered disrespectful to the wife?" I ask incredulously.

"My parents were raised in a religion that offers confession," he answers carefully.

"Ah, I see. Sin first, ask for forgiveness later?"

"Something like that."

"Look, Juan," I say, sitting up straighter, "I don't consider that respectful. Maybe we shouldn't mention our engagement just yet. Not until we can agree on the terms of our relationship."

He looks panicked.

"Driver, stop here," he says, escorting me out of the car.

I'm half-worried that he's kicking me to the curb, but he delicately takes my face in his hands.

"Shelby, my love, we must agree now because, upon entering my home, we'll be sharing the good news with my parents. Of this, I am very pleased. So, tell me your hesitations."

"Will there be a prenup?" I ask.

"No, my darling. We will be wed for life, I hope. What is mine is yours. We will live a life of luxury, and you will be my queen."

"What about other women? Will you be faithful in our marriage?"

He closes his eyes and sighs. "I want to be."

"But that is difficult for you to commit to?"

"Honestly, yes, it is. I seem not to be capable of it."

"Juan, respect and truth are more important to me than fidelity. Here's what I propose. At whatever point in our wedded bliss you should desire to take an additional lover, you must tell me about it. For me, it's not the infidelity that is disrespectful; it's the sneaking around and lying. I also would ask that any affairs be discreet—whether we take a lover individually or together."

"Together?" he says, shocked.

"Yes. I am not opposed to being creative in our sex life. I'm not opposed to sharing you with another woman on occasion as well as being shared with another man. But it has to be equal. For example, if you are allowed to take a lover, so am I. We must be honest with each other about it and swear not to go behind each other's backs."

He looks thoroughly perplexed. "The thought of you with another man greatly upsets me, but I will agree to your demands. In the past, I did sneak around. It would be wonderful to have your blessing. It also would probably take the thrill out of it."

"I never thought of it that way," I say, smiling. "But please know that it is my sincerest hope that I am all you will ever want."

"That is my desire as well," he agrees.

"You mentioned that your mother is religious. Will you tell her of my pregnancy today?"

He violently shakes his head. "No, not until after we are married."

"She will be able to do the math once the baby is born. We can't keep that part a secret."

Juan grins. "If she mentions a concern, we will remind her that she and my father married in July, and I was born in January."

I count it out on my fingers. "Six months. So, with your parents, some things are not discussed?"

"Only what is pleasing and pleasant are safe discussions with my mother," he tells me, making me more nervous.

"How did she treat your first wife?" I ask. "Was she nice to her?"

"She was very critical. Vanessa was beautiful. She was strong-willed. And, even though my mother knew we were in love, our union did not produce an heir. Really, the fact that she had a career of her own was why my mother didn't approve of her. She felt that was why our marriage failed—because Vanessa hadn't kept up with her wifely duties. She's a bit old-fashioned."

"So, your mother would prefer that I didn't work?"

"What matters to me is what *you* want. If you choose to work, I will give you my full support, but there is no financial need. And, honestly, I would rather you be available to travel with me, to spend your afternoons lunching with friends, or to help support charitable organizations. You will be seen in society, and your personal upkeep will be a chore as well."

"Like working out? Are you saying you won't love me if I get fat? You know I'm going to get bigger as my pregnancy progresses, right?"

"Of course I do, my darling. I promise to love you, providing you promise to love yourself."

"Well, if you think I'm letting this body go to pot, you've got another thing coming."

"I hope it is *me* who has you *coming*, my darling. Are you still willing to take my hand in marriage?"

I let out a little huff but am very pleased. No job? Doing nothing but lunching, shopping, traveling, and working out? Yeah, sign me up.

"Yes, I am."

"It is settled then," he says, sealing the deal with a kiss.

"Not exactly. We need to discuss my pregnancy. When we do announce that we are pregnant, your mother will ask about the timing. Like were you even near California when the baby was conceived? When people ask when and how we met, what will we say?"

"Hmm. We will tell the truth about how and where we met, but we will fudge the dates a little. Approximately when did you conceive?"

"Um"—I take my phone out of my pocket, noticing Riley has texted and called numerous times, and look at my calendar—"I got pregnant on August the twenty-fourth."

He pulls out his phone and smiles. "We are clearly meant to be. I had a match in San Diego the week after and actually did stay at the hotel where we met on that date. After that, I kept finding myself wanting to spend more time with you. I just proposed to you on my yacht. Anything else?"

With no prenup and the ability to fuck around if I desire, I don't see any reason to wait. "Juan, when would you like to marry?"

"As soon as you can plan it," he replies.

"I was just thinking about what you said about your mother. With me being pregnant and my not wanting to make a bad impression before we are married, we probably need to do it soon."

"The sooner, the better, yes," he agrees.

I tilt my head, pretending like I just thought of something, but in reality, I have been thinking about it since he proposed. "I've heard, sometimes, celebrity couples surprise guests at a party by getting married."

"Are you suggesting we get married this weekend? As part of the festivities?" A tear forms in his eye.

"What's wrong?" I panic.

"Nothing," he says, placing his hand over his heart. "Everything is perfect. My father will pass soon. It could be any day. It would make me very happy for him to die with the knowledge that his company is in good hands and having seen me wed. But I am torn between my own desires and wanting you to plan the wedding of your dreams."

"Juan, you're the man of my dreams. I don't need an extravagant wedding." I point to the castle looming in the distance and can't help but laugh. "Um, maybe because you were born with it, a place like that is just a pile of bricks to you—"

"Stone actually." He laughs.

"But to someone like me, getting married in a castle is a fairy tale come true. I'll just need to find a white dress."

"I will have a designer flown in from Milan," he says.

"And a simple bouquet."

"I will have ten florists at your beck and call. We will hold extravagant receptions at our homes around the world."

I shake my head. "If that's what you want, I will, but it's not what I need."

He kisses my forehead. "What do you need, my dear?"

"I just told you—a white dress, a simple bouquet, and you standing at the end of the aisle. Anything beyond that will be for you."

He pulls me in for a desire-filled kiss. I find myself extremely turned on, my hand immediately moving to the front of his pants to grope him. It doesn't matter that we are on the side of the road. The second I have his pants unzipped and his cock freed, he picks me up, pushes me against the side of the car, and fucks me.

EVEN THOUGH WE have agreed to everything and I've been coached on how to behave, I'm still pretty nervous when I meet his mother. She is tall, stately, and looks much younger than I expected. Of course, women with money have access to the best skin care and plastic surgeons. And I do notice that her forehead seems to be frozen in place. Her lips are plumped, and her body is shapely. She's wearing a suit, nude pantyhose, designer heels, and a matching hat. Not to mention, large, ornate jewelry, none of it appearing to be costume.

I look down at my simply tailored dress. I remember thinking it was the ultimate in high fashion when Riley's personal shopper suggested it.

"Mother, I'd like you to meet Shelby Benson, my betrothed," Juan says.

"Betrothed?" his mother gasps. "You are engaged? To be married?"

"Yes, Mother," Juan replies with a large grin.

I can tell this all makes him happy. *I* make him happy.

"And I hope you will welcome her into our family with open arms, for I am desperately in love with her."

I have never had someone so openly share their love for me, and it makes me feel utterly romantic.

His mother has an amused look on her face, almost like she doesn't quite believe him. But then she takes my hand, observing the massive engagement ring on my finger. "It suits you, dear. Congratulations."

"Thank you," I tell her.

Juan tightly wraps his arm around my waist, and I make sure to stand up straight—chest out and chin up, like the ladies I observed at the hotel. I am so glad that I studied their every move.

She kisses each of our cheeks and then takes my hand. "Juan, you should go to your father while your bride-to-be and I have a talk."

Juan doesn't let go of me, and I can tell that he's nervous about his mother liking me. It's really kind of cute.

"Well, there's more news, Mother. And I hope you will give us your blessing. It will require much work on your part, and I know it is a lot to ask with you having to plan the party as well as care for father."

"What do you wish, my son?" she asks, carefully studying him.

"I do not want to wait to make my beloved my wife. I offered her the wedding of her dreams at any location in the world, but she asked me where I would choose if it were my decision. I told her of my desire to marry here, in the chapel. Of course, I would leave it to the two of you to plan further, but I mentioned how lovely the gardens were. I wondered if you would allow us to marry and have a small gathering of select guests before the parade."

His mother's face, through all her Botox, actually registers shock. "So soon?"

"Yes, Mother, we are very much in love and do not want to dally."

"Very well. Traditionally, the groom does not have much say in the wedding planning, but I know young people are changing that. What do you desire, son?"

He hugs me. "I already have everything I desire. I just want to make it official in the eyes of the church."

"Your bride and I will figure out everything else. Come, my dear," she says to me, "let me show you the gardens."

Juan takes my handbag, tells me it will be delivered to our room, and deeply kisses me. "Until we meet again."

Gawd, he's so freaking romantic.

His mother motions for me to follow her, and even though I am going to plan my wedding, I feel a little like I'm being taken to the principal's office.

In school, they taught us how to know the difference between two words that sounded the same—*principal* and *principle*. They said that our school princi*pal* was our friend. All I know is, that was not a true statement. The man at my school did not give two shits. I didn't want to leave school. I wanted to graduate and go to college, but when I tried to explain why I was absent, been late, or missed a test, he didn't want to hear about my home life or try to help me in any way. And, when he threatened expulsion for my truancy—like I'd wanted to skip school and stay home with my drugged-out-of-her-mind mother—I had to drop out. I was afraid the state would take me if they saw our living conditions, and I'd heard horror stories about that. At least my mother's behavior was consistent. I knew what to expect. Knew how to deal with it. Knew when to hide in my room and be quiet and when not to. I'd learned to shoplift food from a young age just so I could eat.

And, now, I'm standing in a castle with a twenty-five-million-dollar diamond on my finger, and I'm actually in love with the man who put it there.

Really, I owe Riley a thank-you.

Oh, shit. Riley.

I almost forgot about him. I need to message him back. Now.

"Mrs. Martinez, would you mind terribly if I went to our room to briefly freshen up before we got started?"

"Of course not, dear. I'll have Fernando escort you, and he can bring you back when you are ready. That will give me a few moments to speak to my assistant. I assume you don't have a dress?"

"Juan mentioned something about calling someone he knew in Milan to find me a white dress. I have shoes I could wear, so all I need really is a simple bouquet."

"A *simple* bouquet?" She laughs. "Oh, my dear, *that* will not do."

FERNANDO SHOWS ME to my room, which really isn't a bedroom. It's a gorgeous apartment.

I find my purse and check my phone. *Shit.* There are a lot of texts from Riley, wondering where I am.

I call him. "Hey, sorry, my phone wasn't working."

"Where are you?" he asks. "I called the hotel. I was worried about you!"

"Oh, you shouldn't be. I'm fine. Just on an unplanned trip."

"To where?" he demands.

Do I tell him? No. I haven't passed the mother test yet, and really, until Juan and I are actually married, I can't say anything. If this all happens, I'll tell Riley the truth and apologize. Until then, I need to keep him on the hook, just in case. It is really horrible of me, but whatever. A girl has to do what a girl has to do.

"Do you remember my friend, the one I loaned the money to so that she could start her own nail salon? She asked me to come for her grand opening."

"That's fine, Shelby. I just wish you had told me where you would be."

"You didn't tell me where you would be, Riley," I fire back. "I just got a text, saying you were gone."

"Well, that's more than I got. If you must know, I have been in London for a friend's wedding and to celebrate my birthday."

"Oh, Riley, when is your birthday?"

"It was yesterday."

"Well, happy birthday. I hope you had a great day. When will you be back in town?"

"When will *you* be back?" he asks in a snippy tone.

"Probably not until next week. You?"

"Monday. Just message me when you get back, and we'll reschedule our dinner," he says. "I'm sorry I'm being a dick. I was just worried about you and the baby. Don't just up and leave again like that."

I feel a pang of guilt. No doubt I'm going to hell for lying to him, but as I look at the gilded four-poster bed and the luxurious furnishings, I decide it's worth it.

"I won't, Riley. I'm sorry."

I quickly hang up, take a pee, make sure my nose isn't shiny, and then leave the room, taking my handbag with me this time. I'd like to stay and check it all out, but I don't want to piss his mother off by keeping her waiting. A butler—no, she referred to him as a *footman*; whatever that is—is waiting outside the door for me, like it's his job.

I'm following him through the castle to an expansive terrace overlooking a beautiful garden when I realize it actually is his job.

On the terrace, I see that Juan's mother has been joined by another woman.

She quickly introduces us. "Shelby, I'd like you to meet my personal secretary, Rosario. I've informed her of the news."

"Congratulations," Rosario says. She then proceeds to run through so many options that it makes my head spin. I often ask Mrs. Martinez for her opinion and defer to it because I don't have a freaking clue. Really, about the only input I offer up is that my favorite color is pink.

That causes Juan's mother to clap. "Are you sure you don't understand the Day of the Dead traditions?" she inquires.

"Not really. Where I'm from, we just celebrate Halloween. But I was baptized and given first communion in the Catholic church"—back when my grandmother was alive and took me to church every Sunday—"and we always went to mass on All Saints' Day. Although, once, I went to a parade in Los Angeles that had a lot of skulls and stuff."

Juan's mother smiles at me, seemingly thrilled that we share the same religion. I don't bother to mention that I haven't been to church since my grandmother died when I was nine.

Another household employee—this one dressed in all white, including gloves, and deemed the underbutler, which I think means he's below the butler in the house hierarchy—brings a bucket filled with ice and a bottle of vintage champagne. She rattles off the titles of some other staff, but I'm too busy taking it all in.

"We must toast to my future daughter-in-law," Mrs. Martinez says. She raises her glass. "*Salud.*"

I hesitate for a moment, knowing I shouldn't drink.

I notice her closely watching me, so I take a sip and offer a dazzling smile. I am a beaming very-soon-to-be bride.

"Well, you will be happy to know that pink flowers mean celebration and are a very important part of the Day of the Dead, and we will use them in abundance."

THURSDAY, OCTOBER 30TH
BAM'S CASTLE – TURIN, ITALY
Shelby

"MY DEAR, IF you are going to be my daughter, I need you to be candid with me," Juan's mother says. "I can't help but have noticed that you don't drink alcohol. Are you a teetotaler, or are you with child?"

"My mother was an addict, so I don't drink much," I reply.

She raises an eyebrow at me. Based on the amount of work she's had done to her face, I know this takes effort.

"I don't want to be dishonest with you. That's not the way I want to start off our relationship when you have been so generous with your time regarding our wedding. But I also don't want to offend you or go against Juan's wishes."

"How would you offend me?" she asks.

"Because of our religious beliefs," I say gently.

She laughs. "Darling, my own marriage took place in July, and Juan was born in January. I'm afraid our passion could not wait until we were married. My being pregnant is why we got married, although I fiercely loved him."

"Fiercely." I nod. "That is the perfect word to describe how I feel about your son. I admit to very humble beginnings, and honestly, I didn't want to accept this ring. I would have been just as happy if he had given me a plastic one. I only want his love. For our wedding, I want to do what makes your family happy. All I care about is marrying him in the church."

"What about your family, dear?"

I don't tell her about my mother. It's not that part of me doesn't still love her, but I lied to Riley. She hasn't gotten her life together and probably never will. And she never really wanted me to begin with.

"My grandmother and I were close, but she passed away when I was young. My mother and I are estranged, and it's best that way. She has a toxic personality, and after I moved away from home as a teen, I've never gone back. I've spoken to her, but unfortunately, she has no desire to be part of my life."

Mrs. Martinez pulls me into her arms and gives me a motherly hug. And it's really nice.

"You have a family now. Tonight, you will meet Juan's brothers and sisters and nieces and nephews. I have five children, and all but Juan are married with families. If you tell me that you are indeed with child, regardless of your marriage status, you will make me the happiest woman in the world."

I get tears in my eyes. Finally, someone who is excited about my pregnancy. "I am with child."

"And how far along are you?"

"Twelve weeks on Sunday." I grab my ultrasound photo. I did actually go to the doctor. "Things are progressing well."

I hand her the photo. As she stares at it, her eyes become shiny.

"I'm very happy for you both. When does my son intend to an-nounce this?"

"He wants to wait until after the wedding."

Tears gather in her eyes, but she has yet to blink, not allowing them to fall. "As I'm sure you know, Juan's father is gravely ill. It is his dying wish that all his children be married and have children of their own. Would you please talk to Juan and ask him to reconsider? If it is announced tonight at dinner, no matter when he passes on, it will be with joy in his heart."

Tears fill my eyes as she tightly squeezes my hand. "I will ask, and if he disagrees"—I smile—"maybe I will *accidentally* let it slip."

She laughs through her tears. "That is how many a wife gets her way in life. When my husband passes, Juan will take on a great responsibility."

"I know. He told me."

"Does he seem to have any regrets?"

"Only one. He loves playing polo. You can see it in his eyes when he speaks of it. As someone who loves him, I worry that he will regret leaving the game he has spent his lifetime perfecting. But he greatly values his family and will do what he must."

"I see," she says curtly.

Shit. Maybe I shouldn't have told her the truth.

AT DINNER, WHEN all is announced and congratulations are had, we are asked to retire to Juan's parents' sitting room in their large quarters.

"Juan," his mother says once we are all seated, "your father and I have been discussing something I never realized until your love and I spoke of it today."

"What did you speak of?" he asks, his eyes wildly searching mine for answers.

"Your career. You should know that we are very proud of you for pursuing your dreams and what it has led you to accomplish. Honestly, we had thought you to be impetuous because of the game. We often felt jealous that it took you away from us. But your father remembers your first match and the joy written all over your face. We are proud of your pursuit of greatness in your sport. We know that you have sacrificed much in that pursuit, but we thought that it was the cause for you not having children, for seeming not to want to settle down. After meeting Shelby—learning of your desire to marry and her being with child and witnessing your happiness—we realize that we were remarkably incorrect. You had just not met the right woman who was worth settling down for."

"I'm thankful that you are proud of my accomplishments. That means a lot to me," he says.

"We don't want you to retire from the game you love," his father says.

"What do you mean? I must take over the family business."

"We see no reason why you can't do both. For the day-to-day operations of the business, there is a very talented young man running our mining division. I think you are well acquainted."

"Are you referring to Nico?" Juan asks his father.

"Yes. This week, I will be relinquishing my role as chairman of the board to you, my son. I suggest your first order of business is to promote your most trusted friend, Nico, to CEO of our holding company. He can handle the day-to-day operations of our conglomerate while you pursue your passions. If I can give you some advice, Juan, regardless of blood relation, only put those you trust in places of power within your organization. It is of the utmost importance."

Juan looks overwhelmed with emotions as he takes his father's hand, kisses his forehead, and says, "Thank you, Papa."

We bid his parents good night, and when we get back to our room, Juan slams the door shut, pushes me up against it, deeply kisses me, and shoves up the layers of my skirt.

Much later, when we are both physically spent and have finally made our way to the bed, he holds me in his arms and says, "You're the best thing to ever happen to me."

JOHNSON HOME – NEW YORK CITY
Vanessa

"HAPPY LATE BIRTHDAY," I tell Riley when he greets us at his parents' front door.

"Thanks," he says, giving us hugs then taking our coats.

"Where is everyone?" Dawson asks.

"Dad's out back, smoking a cigar. Mom is still at dance class with the girls," Riley tells us, glancing at his watch. "They should be done by now, but Mom was going to take them to dinner. She was worried that if she got back here before we left, the girls would want to go."

"That's true," Dawson says. "Fill us in on your birthday. What did you do? I hope it involved bowling and waffles."

"My actual birthday was pretty low-key but nice. Keatyn had Marvel make chicken and waffles and a confetti birthday cake. Dallas and I went bowling, did a little pub-crawling, and then capped the night off with a great dinner at an iconic London steak house. Left early the next morning, touching down in New York around noon. After I got dropped off, the plane refueled and then took Dallas out west to California."

"And we're very glad it did," I say, grinning. "Thank you for having it bring us here. It's the first time I've had the pleasure of flying in it. And I hope it won't be the last."

"It won't be," Riley says. But then he gets to what's really on his mind. "Are you sure you need to go to this event?"

"We have to go," I answer simply. "It's important to Dawson."

He shakes his head as he moves toward the bar. "Just don't say I didn't warn you."

"Riley," Dawson says, snaking his arm around my waist, "of all people, you ought to know that Vanessa can handle herself in volatile situations. It's part of her job."

"That's right," I say, giving him a sweet kiss. "I can."

But part of me isn't so sure. Going to Dawson's dead wife's fundraiser is sort of the last thing I want to do. But I love him and want to support him. And he's been extremely stressed out and a little snippy the last couple of days. At first, I worried it might be because of my pregnancy, but I think it's because he's been dreading this event.

THE EVENT IS being held in a posh ballroom in a beautiful old hotel with views of Central Park.

As Dawson takes my hand to help me out of the limo, his voice wavers. "Are you sure?"

"Yes, I'm sure. Let me fix your tie first." I slide my hand through the hair at the nape of his neck and pull him closer to me.

"I've never been very good at tying a bow tie."

"Lucky for you, I am. I used to tie my dad's." I undo and then properly retie the bowtie, pulling out the edges of the bow.

Dawson grabs my wrists and gazes into my eyes. "You have no idea how much it means to me that you're here."

"There's nowhere I'd rather be than by your side," I say sincerely as his hands slide down my arms and then one covers my belly.

"Are you sure you're not too tired?"

"I'm fine. I slept with my head in your lap nearly the entire flight here."

"I know," he says with a grin. "It was heavenly."

"You are a charmer," I tell him. "And you look quite handsome."

"I look pretty damn handsome, too, if I do say so myself," Riley interjects. "Let's go do this. The sooner we get in there, the sooner we can get the fuck out."

I notice Dawson and Riley exchange a look.

"What was that all about?" I ask Riley.

"Nothing," he lies. "We were just admiring how fine you look in that red gown."

I narrow my eyes at Dawson, causing him to roll his. "Fine. Riley agreed to take you home early if need be."

"While I find that very sweet, I'm a big girl. If I want to leave, I will. I don't need a chaperone."

ONCE WE WALK into the ballroom, it doesn't take long for Whitney's mother, Mrs. Clarke, to make a beeline for us.

"That's her," Riley says to me. "I'm half-tempted to pretend you are my date, so she doesn't freak out on Dawson."

But I just nod my head and keep my arm tucked under Dawson's elbow.

"Is this the woman you're going to live in sin with?" the woman asks. "What kind of values will that give my granddaughters?"

Riley starts to say something, but Dawson doesn't allow it. "Mrs. Clarke, with all due respect, the values I choose to teach my children are none of your business."

"I disagree wholeheartedly. You're setting a bad example, and I won't stand for it. And what about Whitney? What about their mother?"

"She's dead," I say, causing everyone's mouths to drop open.

Mrs. Clarke narrows her eyes at me and walks away.

"I can't believe you just said that," Riley says. "Go, Vanessa."

"I hope it didn't come off as rude or disrespectful," I say. "I was just stating the obvious."

"Well, it was awesome," Riley says.

But Dawson doesn't look so sure.

THE REST OF the evening goes smoothly. I enjoy meeting the people Dawson used to work with as well as the couples he and Whitney were friends with. All seem genuinely happy to hear that he and the girls are doing well. Other than the run-in with Whitney's mother, I've felt completely welcome at the event.

While Dawson and Riley are engaged in a serious conversation with an old family friend, I step away to get some water. It's starting to get warm in here, and I'm feeling a little flushed.

I'm nearly to the bar when Whitney's mother corners me.

"Why are you here? It's so disrespectful to my daughter's memory," she says.

"I'm here for two reasons," I reply calmly. "The first one being that I'm here to support Dawson."

"And the second?" she snaps.

"Because I can relate," I say softly.

"And just how can you do that?" Her face twists up, making her look ugly.

I don't reply right away. I want my comment to have sufficient weight.

I am silent for a few beats and then finally say, "Because my own mother committed suicide when I was young. I know what it's like to grow up without a mother, and I wouldn't wish it on anyone."

Her face goes slack, but then she steadies herself, putting the bitch face back on. "I'll have you know that my daughter got stuck inside the garage while her car was running. She *never* would have killed herself. And you are disgracing her honor by suggesting otherwise."

"I see," I say quietly and walk away. There's really nothing more I can say. The woman obviously isn't dealing with reality. Or maybe the guilt she feels for not being supportive of her daughter weighs on her, and it's easier to pretend—like my dad did.

"I heard what she said to you," Dawson says, pulling me into his arms. "I appreciate your support more than you know."

"It's really too bad she isn't open about what Whitney did. When you told me that she did a fundraiser every year in her daughter's honor, I just assumed it went to charities that supported those who dealt with depression. I'm also surprised you've never teamed up with Moon Wish."

"It's just how she is. She was hard on Whitney and was always comparing her to her older sister. Whitney never felt good enough, which certainly wasn't the cause of her depression, but it didn't help matters. As for teaming up, honestly, I have barely been able to deal with my own family for the last couple of years."

"Does that mean you don't have any say?"

"In where the money goes?" he asks.

"Yes." I turn and ask the bartender for a glass of water.

As I take a sip, Dawson says, "Whitney's grandfather set up the foundation and made me the trustee, but for the past two years, Whitney's mom has told me how to allocate the funds."

"Maybe out of respect for your late wife, you *shouldn't* do what her mother tells you."

Dawson smiles at me, nodding his head. "You're amazing."

"That, I know." I smirk. "But am I right? I'm good at PR. We could do big things with it, if that's something you want. But I don't want to push you to do something you aren't comfortable with. I also think your girls need to understand. Understand what happened. Understand the disease. Be able to help the cause."

"You're right about everything," he says.

He's deep in thought when Whitney's mother takes the stage.

She speaks fondly of her late daughter before calling up Dawson.

I have to give him a little nudge with my elbow.

"Shit," he mutters as he realizes it's time for him to take his place behind the podium.

He makes his way to the front of the room and gives a brief overview of the causes the foundation donated money to this past year, using a few notecards as his guide, but then he sets the cards down, steps out from behind the podium, and paces across the stage.

"This is usually the point in my speech where I tell you about our goals for the coming year, but . . ." He runs his hand back through his hair, seemingly struggling to keep his composure. "The first time we gathered for this event, it was only a month after Whitney's death, and the pain was very fresh. I could barely believe she was gone.

"Over the course of the last two years, I've struggled with grief and guilt. I've struggled with the realities of being a single parent. I quit a job I loved and immersed myself in my girls' lives because I thought they needed me. But, looking back, I realize I needed them.

"I know we've all been in your prayers. I know you all wonder how we've been coping. How the girls are. How her parents are. I want to tell you that, slowly, we're healing. And, as I took the stage tonight, I realized that, even though this event was created to celebrate Whitney's life, it's been more about those she left behind.

"Tonight, I want to change that. I want to honor her memory. My wife was smart and beautiful and confident. She fiercely loved our children. And we need to honor her with truth.

"I first fell in love with Whitney when I was just fourteen, a freshman at boarding school. She was magnetic and graceful, and if I had to describe her in one word, it would be that she had *presence*. On the surface, she had it all.

"As the trustee of her foundation as well as the man who loved her for much of his life, I need to tell you something. I need to tell you the truth. I need to tell you about the Whitney you didn't know because not bringing to light why she died means we aren't doing our part. What many of you don't know is that Whitney struggled with depression.

"When she was a senior in high school, she tried to commit suicide. Whatever you have been told about Whitney's death, I'm sure we can all agree it was senseless. But the fact that it wasn't accidental makes it even more so. Whitney *wanted* to die. Just think about that for a minute. This beautiful woman who had a wonderful life and a loving family wanted to die.

"We all have struggles. There were times I wished I could disappear, but on the very few times that thought crossed my mind, it would quickly be replaced with rational thoughts, like knowing I could never do that to my family. Maybe that rational thought happened because I'd never really been in that much pain.

"Whitney was on medication, but there were good and bad days, lots of ups and downs. Many of you know that Whitney's brother-in-law was recently sentenced to many years in prison. You have all probably seen the papers and know how much money he lost. What you don't know is that Whitney invested everything we had with him. And she lost it all—my retirement fund and the monies from my trust, her trust. All of it was wiped out.

"As all of us do when we lose money, we feel pretty badly, but after the initial shock and outrage, we do what humans do best. We persevere, we adjust our lifestyle, we work harder to earn more, we figure something out.

"But it doesn't work that way for a person who is already struggling with depression. She didn't tell me the extent of the loss, only admitted to taking a little hit in our portfolio. For months, she hid the truth from me. It wasn't until the bank was threatening foreclosure on our house because she hadn't been making the payments did she tell me. I was pissed. Understandably upset. I couldn't believe she had risked our future like that. I stormed off, but once I got over the initial shock, I began to take action. I told her it would be okay. That we'd figure it out. At that point, it was like a weight had lifted from her shoulders.

"For one week, everything was good. She seemed happy. But she wasn't.

"On the day she passed, she sent our children to my parents' for the night, so we could share a romantic evening together. Only, when I got home, I found her in the garage—with the car running."

He stops, gets his wallet out of his suit jacket, and pulls out a folded up piece of paper.

"This is the note that she left. I've carried it with me every day since to remind myself that, no matter how bad things might seem, life is precious. I'd like to read to you what she said."

He unfolds the paper. "*My dearest Dawson, I once read that suicide is selfish. That, by taking my life, I'll be leaving you to clean up the mess— literally, financially, and emotionally. I'm sorry for the pain this will cause you, but your love for me is what's gotten me through for as long as it has. You don't deserve this. Our sweet girls don't deserve this. But I know, in the long run, you will all be better off without having to deal with the sadness I perpetually carry in my heart. Please don't tell the girls that I took my own life. Please don't let them question my love, for it's my love for them that makes this right.*"

Tears stream down my face as he speaks, and I understand even more why this has been so hard for him—because he's been forced to lie about it.

He wipes the tears from his face, folds the paper back up, and slips it back into his wallet. "I blamed myself. I should have seen the signs. I should have known. I should have stopped it.

"Since then, for nearly two full years, I've focused my life solely on the one thing that was important to her—our children. My family told me that I had to get over it. I had to start living my life. That I wasn't actually setting a good example for my children.

"Last month, an old friend offered me a position in California. I met an amazing woman who lost her own mother to suicide and who helped me understand that I need to let go of the guilt. Starting today, I'm doing just that.

"The money we raise tonight will honor Whitney in a different way—by being truthful about why she died rather than covering it up. We'll be teaming up with Moon Wish Wine to help spread the word about depression and its dangers and to create resources for families. If we can stop just *one* mother from taking her own life, then I will not just be taking care of Whitney's children, as she wanted me to do, but other children. Thank you so much for your continued support."

He lowers his head and takes a deep breath, and the music starts playing again.

"They're lies. All lies!" Whitney's mother screams out, breaking down and dramatically dropping to the floor.

Dawson rushes to help her.

"Don't you touch me!" she yells. "You were a horrible husband and are a horrible father. I will sue you for defamation. For custody of your children! You'll never see them again! You don't deserve them! You will not ruin my daughter's good name with this nonsense. You're fired from the foundation."

Dawson stands there in horror. The moving speech he just gave, quickly forgotten.

A good-looking, tall, older gentleman, whom I have yet to meet, gets into the fray. I don't know who he is, but he has presence.

"You wouldn't face the truth about our daughter's depression during her life," he says to Mrs. Clarke, pulling her upright. "Now, you don't have a choice." He turns to Dawson and shakes his hand. "I'm proud of you, son. It took courage to do what you just did, and I fully support you." He gives Mrs. Clarke a glare. "And I won't let my ex-wife stand in your way."

"WELL, THAT WAS an exciting night," Riley says later as we get in the car that will be taking us back to their parents' home.

"I still feel bad that I upset Mrs. Clarke," Dawson says, running his hand back through his hair with a sigh.

"She's an old bitch," Riley counters. "She deserved it."

"No, she didn't, Riley," I say. "She's a mother who lost her daughter. She's still in pain."

I run my hand down Dawson's arm, comforting him. Regardless of how well he seemed to handle things, I can tell he's a mess inside—something his brother is too stupid to see.

"I thought you handled it well, Dawson. Maybe upsetting her this one time will help her face the truth. Maybe she'll turn out to be your biggest supporter. Maybe she just needed her world flipped to reality."

"That would be nice," he says softly. "And, if she wants to see her grandchildren, she's going to have to shape up."

WHEN WE GET home, Dawson pulls me into the bedroom and kisses me hard.

"Thank you," he says.

"Oh, thank you," I reply, grinning. "What did I do to deserve a kiss like that?"

"Because you flipped my world to a wonderful reality. Thank you again for coming with me tonight. For being by my side."

"I love you, Dawson. *By your side* is exactly where I should be."

He slips the strap of my dress off my shoulder and delicately runs his hand down my spine. "And I was thinking, *in*side you is exactly where I should be."

FRIDAY, OCTOBER 31ST
BAM'S CASTLE – TURIN, ITALY

Shelby

IT'S HALLOWEEN, A holiday I never cared for—mostly because I could never afford a costume. But this Halloween is different. I feel like I'm inside a fairytale—living in a castle, wearing an elaborate off-the-shoulder designer gown with a fitted waist and a sweeping, full skirt in a soft, shimmering pink ombre, and going to a masked ball. I made Juan leave before he saw my dress, thinking of how utterly romantic it will be when he first catches a glimpse of me.

I pick up my skirt so I don't trip and make my way to the ballroom. It's like nothing I've ever seen before, not even in the movies. Who goes to a masked ball on Halloween in a real castle?

Me, apparently. I can't help but grin as I float through the room searching for my love, but I discover he's hard to find. While the women's dress styles vary widely, the men are a little harder to tell apart.

I assumed Juan would be at my side the second I stepped into the room, but I also know that the anticipation of him finding me is a huge turn on. I step in front of a large banquet table filled with more food than I've ever seen in one place and am contemplating where to start when Juan's sister, Nina, comes up next to me and says, "I suggest you starve yourself before the wedding, or you'll never fit into your dress."

"Why would I do that?" Of all of Juan's family, Nina seems to have a chip on her shoulder. You'd think a woman used to such wealth and excess would never want for anything and would be perpetually happy, but she's not. She's catty and underhanded. I'm pretty sure when Juan's father spoke last night of trusting people in business, he was warning him about Nina's disruptive personality. "I have a fast metabolism and I've always been able to eat whatever I want. I guess I'm just lucky," I say, letting my eyes wander to Nina's midsection, which is a bit thick.

"How old are you?" she asks.

"Twenty-three. Why?"

"Your body is fake." She scrunches up her nose at me in disgust. Which is sort of funny, considering the amount of plastic surgery her mother has surely had. And based on the frown lines across her forehead because of her perpetual scowl, I'm betting she'll be the next in line for the plastic surgeon.

I look down at my boobs, assuming that's what she is referring to. "Actually, Nina, there is nothing on me that isn't God given. And there is not an ounce of flab on my body. I work hard and eat healthy to insure that. Hashtag blessed."

"Yeah, right," she snaps. "Bam's ex-wife was rail thin and his last girlfriend was a super model."

"I'll have you know that I've worn numerous designer gowns"— okay, really three, but she doesn't need to know that—"on the red carpet. They fit quite lovely."

"Then you are a gold digger. I don't know how you managed to get your claws into my brother, but I don't like you. And I speak for my entire family."

"Actually," I say with a smirk, "if I understand correctly, it is *you* who is a gold digger."

She's taken aback and puts her hand up to her flat chest. "How can you even say that? I was born into—"

"Your family owns a gold mine, correct?"

"Yes," she mutters, still looking perplexed.

"And how do they get it out of the mine?" I ask.

"They excavate it."

"Exactly. They *dig*. That makes your family gold diggers, literally."

I hear Juan burst out in laughter. "Just one of the many reasons I am in love with you," he says, wrapping his arms around me before turning his attention to his sister. "Nina, what you said to my future bride was inappropriate and rude. Apologize immediately." He looks at his sister with contempt.

"I call them as I see them. And if you think you can come in and take over the business that you've never paid any attention to your whole life, you're wrong."

Juan releases me, strides toward his sister, and grabs her arm tightly. He does nothing but stare at her for a few moments. Then he says, "You will respect me as head of the family as well as my wife. And if you don't, not only will you *not* have a job, I will see to it that you and your free-spending husband don't get another peso, dollar, franc, or euro. Are we clear?"

She lowers her head and mutters, "Yes, brother."

"What else do you have to say, Nina?"

"Sorry for what I said," she says, glaring at me. It's obvious she doesn't mean it. She hates me and wants me to know it.

"You are dismissed, Nina," Juan says as she retreats to a corner of the ballroom.

"Your sister hates me. It's sad, really. I used to dream of having a sister. Thought it would be so fun. I'm thinking I was wrong."

"It is not you. She's mad at me."

"Because you are going to take over the company and she works there and thinks she knows it all?"

"Exactly, which is humorous since she is not even in a position of power."

"And you get the best of both worlds. You get to continue playing the game you love as well as run the company. Although, I didn't really understand what your father meant by the holding company."

"We are a multinational conglomerate. Our family could never run something so large on our own. We have trusted employees in places of power and we pay them handsomely. My father reviews reports and has traveled the world checking in on different divisions, but it's because of his keen eye for quickly deducing a person's abilities that the company has grown into what it has. I but only have to, as you say, keep the wheels on the wagon. Each company has their own management hierarchy and most are publicly traded. The holding company that I will serve as chairman of, does just what it sounds like, we own—or hold—the majority of stock in the individual companies. We guide each company and try to make it more profitable, which then makes the stocks worth more as well as increases our net worth."

"Can we sit for a minute, Juan?" I say, not bothering to wait for his reply. I take a seat, feeling flush and like I may faint.

"Are you okay?" he asks, sitting next to me and taking my hand in his.

"I'm feeling a little shaken. I think I need something to eat."

"I will be right back." He rushes over to the buffet, quickly filling a plate and bringing it to me. "You must be sure to eat during the festivities. You're growing a baby and need extra calories."

I pop a piece of focaccia in my mouth and drink some water then proceed to demolish everything on the plate. When I'm finished, I let out a contented yawn.

"My dear," he says. "We must share a dance, then I am going to take you back to our suite to rest."

THE WHOLE TIME we're dancing I can feel Nina throwing daggers at me with her eyes. Maybe this isn't going to work. When we get back to our suite, I sit on the bed.

"Juan, what will our married life be like? Where will we live?" I'm still feeling a little shaken. "I'm not used to dealing with family. I left my family because they didn't treat me well. I won't go through that again."

"I will not allow my sister to treat you with anything other than respect."

"All that means is when you are around she will be nice, but when you aren't, she will try to undermine me at every turn. She's a liar, Juan. You can see it in her eyes."

"And you are very astute. She's always been a liar, since childhood. It seems you have my father's gift for judging a person's character." He sits on the bed next to me and kisses me, distracting me by sliding his hand across the front of my dress. "I love your breasts, by the way, and know innately that you were most definitely blessed."

"Everyone always thinks they are fake, but I never had the money to buy fake boobs."

"My darling, you now have the money to buy anything your heart desires."

"And I already told you I don't desire anything but you." I start unbuttoning his shirt.

"Now?"

"Yes, but I'd like you to fully answer my question first. How will we live?"

"Famously," he says, quickly unzipping the back of my gown.

"You're going to have to be more specific than that. You mentioned a castle in Argentina. You told me your family lives there. Does that include Nina?"

"Yes, she and her family currently live there. It's where my stables are and where I train. We each have our own homes within the castle grounds. I also have homes of my own around the world. We will be based out of Argentina, but will probably only spend half of our life there. And if the castle doesn't suit you for while we are there, I will make it suitable for you, even if it means relocating my sister. Let's talk of something more pleasant," he says, getting me out of my gown. "Where do you wish to honeymoon? Anywhere in the world."

"I haven't been anywhere in the world, Juan. Where would you like to take me?"

"Well," he says, removing my panties and tossing them aside. "You will need a new wardrobe, first of all. The wives of polo players are typically not seen in public in the same thing twice. I have a few more matches before the end of the year, most of them in Argentina. You will get to see me play—that I cannot wait for. We'll start our honeymoon with a shopping spree. Which would you prefer? Milan, Dubai or Paris?"

"Oh, Dubai sounds so exotic."

"Perfect. Then we will need some time to relax. Let's go to the Maldives. It's not far from Dubai. Would you prefer a beachfront villa or a water villa?"

"Is a water villa the kind that sits on stilts over the water?" I ask.

"Yes."

"Oh, that kind, please. Juan, you are spoiling me," I say with a moan as he slips one finger inside me. "It makes me feel guilty."

"It shouldn't," he replies with a kiss.

"But there are so many people in the world who need help more than I need designer clothing."

He stops what he's doing and smiles at me, pulling me onto his lap. "I have a charity foundation. Would you help me decide on worthy causes?"

"Really? I'd love that. It is so sweet that you want to spoil me, but I don't need it." I mean, I do, but I have just learned that there is actually such a thing as having *too much* money. And I'm pretty sure Juan and his family fall into that category. When I met Riley, I just wanted a few pretty outfits and not to have my rent check bounce.

"Actually, you do need it. Being my wife, people will expect you to present yourself in a certain way."

"A designer-clad way?" I push his shirt off and take one of his nipples into my mouth.

"Yes. Can you live with that?" he replies as he moves on top of me.

I look up at the centuries old, wood-beamed ceiling, feeling a little like I've slipped into some twilight zone.

"As long as we can balance it with giving, I will do my best to represent you. To not embarrass you."

He holds my eyes as he slips inside me. "That you will never do. You will always bask in the luxury of my love and, tomorrow, you will become my wife."

AFTER A FEW hours of "rest", I'm putting on the second of five dresses that I will be wearing over the course of the next few days.

"Hurry," Juan says from the living room. "We shouldn't be late for the feast."

I step out into the room, my dress glittering. Really, all of me is glittering. I literally pinched myself when I was in the dressing room putting it on.

"Will you zip me, please?" I ask, turning my back to him.

"Mhm," he says, lowering his lips to my exposed shoulder. "This dress is like a confection, making me long to taste you again."

"Isn't it gorgeous?" I say, twirling happily in a barely-there pale pink gown infused with golden glitter. Its strapless neckline manages to both cover and uplift my boobs which are further enhanced by a jewel-encrusted empire waistline. This dress is much softer and more comfortable for dinner, but still utterly beautiful. On my feet are gold glittered sandals that are by—damn, now I can't remember the name, but anyone who's anyone would recognize the distinctive red sole.

"It is quite lovely, but I think it needs something. Did the stylist not leave a suitable necklace to wear?"

I frown. "I don't think so. I can go look again."

Juan smiles at me and holds up a large velvet box. "I'm afraid it was planned that way." He opens the box. "My mother thought you might like to borrow this."

I teeter over, the narrow heels feeling dangerous on this old stone floor. Then my eyes widen at the jewels inside.

"Is that real?" I ask, then realize it was a dumb question. I shake my head and smile at Juan. "I suppose your family doesn't wear costume jewelry?"

"Not often. Our company is known for its fine jewels and our family must set a good example. Many of the people invited to dinner are, in fact, business associates."

"Well, then I guess you talked me into wearing it," I tease.

He places a kiss on my matte pink lips then fastens it around my neck.

"Because I know someone will ask," he says, "this is a seven carat pear-shaped yellow diamond."

"Yellow? But it looks golden."

"Because of its cut. This cut is called a fancy vivid, and along with the pear shape helps to intensify the natural color of the stone."

"And it's set in rose gold. It almost looks like it was made for the dress."

"Knowing my mother, it probably was." Juan laughs. "Rumor has it, she keeps a gem cutter and jeweler locked in her closet."

Either is fine with me, I think, as I admire myself in the mirror.

JOHNSON HOME – THE HAMPTONS

Riley

I'M AT ONE of my favorite places in the world. The Hamptons. Most people love it because of its glitzy seaside mansions and quaint small-town feel. But, for me, the Hamptons is all about family.

This home belonged to my grandparents and has been enjoyed by my parents and then their children. With big families, the house started to seem too small, and we couldn't all stay here at the same time. Over the last ten years, we were able to acquire the properties on either side of us, giving us more space to spread out when my father's siblings, their children, and grandchildren get together—like we all will this weekend.

I'm currently sitting out on the deck in the dark by myself, enjoying a few peaceful moments of listening to the ocean waves. Once everyone arrives—either late tonight or early tomorrow—it will be completely chaotic.

After seeing Dawson's girls in their Halloween costumes, I brought my parents out here by helicopter, and we had a quiet dinner together. I can't remember the last time I got to dine with my parents all by myself. And our conversation about passion in life and love was exactly what I needed. I know I'm headed in the right direction. I know what I want to do with my life.

"You hiding out here because you're in trouble with Mom and Dad?" Camden, my oldest brother, asks as he sets a bucket of beers down on the side table next to me.

I get up and give him a hug. I don't see him nearly enough. He and his wife live in Connecticut, have three small boys, and each has their own career.

"Where are the boys and Annie?" I ask.

"The boys had parties at school today and trick-or-treated their little hearts out tonight. And they didn't sleep at all on the way here. They were pretty pumped about their first helicopter ride. You spoil them."

I shrug. "Actually, I was spoiling Annie. I can't imagine the hell a three-hour car ride would have been with three exhausted kids."

He hands me a beer and raises his toward me. "Here's to not having to endure that. What are you doing out here by yourself?"

"Just listening to the ocean. Chilling."

"Bullshit. You don't know how to relax anymore."

"What can I say? I've turned twenty-nine, and all of a sudden, I can."

"Not to mention, you sold your company for a shit-ton of money. Congrats on that, and happy birthday, bro."

"Thanks."

He quickly downs two beers and then attempts to ease into a conversation about my love life. "I hear Annie is helping Ariela with her divorce."

"I don't know much about that side of things. Ariela and I haven't really discussed it, but I know she retained Annie, and they have filed."

He gives me a smirk. "Yeah, well, I suppose juggling two women has been keeping you busy."

When I don't reply to his chiding, he goes, "What the fuck happened? Is this waitress really pregnant? And have you told Mom and

Dad?"

"Not yet. I'm waiting to make sure it's mine first."

"That's not what Dallas said. He said you can't make up your mind and that you've been fucking both Ariela and the baby mama. What is her name again? Shelly?"

"Shelby," I correct.

"Is that really all you're going to say about the matter?" he asks. It kills him, not knowing everything.

"Pretty much. There's not much to talk about."

"Other than she is trying to rope you into marrying her. Please, don't put the family through what we went through with Dawson and Whitney."

"I'm not going to abandon my child," I say simply.

He goes on a tirade about Whitney, about how Shelby is probably just like her, and then starts praising Ariela—which I find humorous since she's still married. But it's quite clear whom my brother favors. But he's never met Shelby.

"It's gotten colder than a witch's tit out here," I say finally. "Let's go inside."

"Well, it is Halloween!" Camden laughs. "I guess that's fitting. Reminds me of when we were at school and used to freeze our asses off sneaking out to smoke at the Cave." He continues reminiscing about his glory days at Eastbrooke. I try not to act bored.

Once I'm half-frozen to death, I herd him inside.

"Looking back, I might have been a bit of an ass in high school," he says as we come into the family room through the sliding doors.

"College, too," Annie yells out, coming down the stairs with a crying child in tow. "I'm raising the white flag. I need wine."

"Coming right up," Camden says, detouring into the kitchen.

"Uncle Riley!" Sutton, their middle child, yells out and miraculously stops crying.

"It's late," Annie says. "Don't get him all wound—"

But it's too late. Wound up is what Uncle Riley does best.

The crier, Sutton, jumps over the banister and leaps toward me, karate-chopping at my arm. I snatch him midair and then roll him onto the couch, pinning him down and tickling his sides as he laughs and kicks at me.

"Up," Annie finishes.

"Uncle Riley!" I hear yelled out as a blur races down the stairs.

A little spider monkey of a child, their youngest son, Callan, pounces on my back. I grab him, so he won't fall off. Then I twist around and lean over, dropping him on the other couch.

Sutton jumps up and launches himself over the large ottoman and onto my shoulder.

Pretty soon, each boy has one of my arms, and they are trying to break me in half by pulling me in opposite directions. Camden gets into the fray, holding me down.

"Boys," Annie says calmly, wine glass in hand, "you're going to rip Uncle Riley's arms off, and then Grandma will not be happy, which will mean no ice cream for you this weekend."

The boys defiantly look at her, eyes narrowed, trying to judge her seriousness.

"She's right," my mother says, coming out of the master bedroom in her robe. "You also need to get your butts to bed. It's late. You're being quite loud, and Grandma is tired. And, if Grandma is tired tomorrow, she won't have the energy to make any of your favorite treats. Plus, Uncle Riley needs his arms to give his mother a good-night hug."

The boys might not listen to Annie all the time, but they know better than to disobey Grandma, especially when treats are involved. They hop to attention, letting go of my arms, and sit next to each other on the couch, pretending to be angels.

"Can we have some ice cream before bed?" Parker, the oldest of the bunch, says from atop the stairs. "You always say milk helps us sleep better."

"You've got me there," Mom says. "Come on down, and we'll have a quick bedtime snack."

Annie rolls her eyes and takes a big gulp of wine. "You have no idea the amount of sugar these boys consumed today."

"Of course I do." Mom smiles, leading the boys into the kitchen. "I raised four of my own."

Camden is still sitting on top of me. Apparently, he doesn't want ice cream. I take the opportunity to reach up and grab him behind his neck. Using my body weight, I roll him over my shoulder and flat onto his back.

"Ugh," he says, hitting the hardwood floor.

"Boys!" Mom screeches. "At least try to set a good example for the younger generation."

But then our younger brother, Braxton, comes through the front door and launches himself on both of us, causing the little boys to ditch their ice cream and get back into the mix—all of us wrestling.

A few minutes later, Camden shoves Braxton, causing him to fall backward and hit his elbow hard on the floor.

"Fuck, that hurt," Braxton says, cradling his arm, as Camden leaps on top of him, pinning him to the ground. "Mom," he cries out, "tell them to stop!"

Camden gets up and looks at me, and we both start laughing.

"Just like always," Camden says with a smirk, "little pussy ends up crying to Mommy."

"Uncle Brax is a little pussy," Sutton says, laughing.

There is a chorus of, "Little pussy," from the boys.

"Do *not* say that word," Annie sternly tells them.

"Does that mean we can say *fuck*?" Parker asks innocently.

Annie glares at Braxton, who is pacing and muttering.

"Hit my fucking funny bone. Stop laughing." He points his finger at Camden and me.

"What is it about this place that turns them all into little kids?" Annie mutters to herself.

Callan jumps up and glares at his mother. "Ain't nothing *little* about a Johnson."

"That's for fucking sure," Braxton says, high-fiving the kid with his good arm.

"Language," our mother says.

"Braxton," my father's voice booms, "you've been here all of five minutes, and the place looks like you had an all-night rager—or whatever those parties are called."

I smile, thinking back to the parties we used to have. The girls, the Hamptons' Kool-Aid. How I couldn't wait until I was old enough to come here without my parents. It was a rite of passage. All of us, except for Braxton, lost our virginity on this beach. Our summers were filled with long days full of sun, surf, girls, and booze. But all of that changed after I started dating Ariela. The summer before my senior year was spent mostly in California, with her, making Captive Film's first movie.

"Excuse me," I say, getting up and going back outside.

I take a walk down the beach, and once I'm a comfortable distance from the house, I take my phone out and call her.

"Riley," she says. "Happy birthday. It's a little late, I know, but you didn't call me back."

"Sorry. Things have been a whirlwind. You sound happy though."

"I am, Riley. Working here is so fun. The weather is gorgeous. The air smells so fresh."

"Does that mean you're definitely staying?" I ask.

"Yes," she says. I don't know why, but I release a breath of air. One that I feel like I've been holding since she walked back into my life.

"That makes me happy, Ariela. There's something I wanted to talk to you about. There's this house that I'm thinking about buying myself for my birthday."

"Where is it?"

"Near the vineyard. I looked at it, and I thought it was great. It needs a little updating, but the grounds are beautiful. I just wondered if you, um, would give me a woman's opinion—"

"If you wanted a woman's opinion, you'd ask Keatyn," she interrupts.

"Keatyn is biased. She wants me to buy it."

"Why?" she asks. "You have a beautiful penthouse in a great location."

"Did you really look at it—like when you were there?"

"No, Riley, I guess I didn't." She lets out a sigh. "All I cared about was you—until Shelby popped out of nowhere."

I ignore her Shelby comment, not wanting it to derail the conversation just yet. "It's got a beautiful view, but it feels a little cold sometimes."

"Riley, a big house in wine country isn't going to fix the fact that you're alone."

"Fine. I was thinking, on the off chance that we could end up living there together, it would be nice if you didn't hate the place."

"Is Shelby giving you her opinion, too?"

"No," I say brusquely.

She's quiet for a moment. A moment that's almost too long. One that stretches like the sea. I hate when she pauses like this. It usually means I won't like her answer.

"I'd love to see it with you, Riley. Thank you for asking."

"Marry me," I blurt out. *Where the fuck did that come from?*

"No," she replies adamantly.

"Why not?" I feel like I'm back at graduation, my heart breaking into little pieces.

"Because you're being impetuous, just like you were on the school lawn the first time you asked me. And we have a lot of things to work out before I could ever say yes."

"Any chance you could come to New York? Like, now?"

"For what?"

"Me," I say softly, barely able to get the words out.

"What are you saying, Riley?"

"I'm saying I'm sorry. Sorry about Shelby and about the way I've been acting. I've done a lot of thinking over the last few days."

"And a lot of drinking from what I understand," she counters.

She must have heard about the bachelor party from Maggie.

"Yes, some of that, too. And I miss you. Desperately."

"I miss you, too, but I still—"

"I agree to your terms, Ariela. Well, sort of."

"Sort of?" she asks.

"I'm not going to be monogamous. I'm going to be celibate."

She lets out a laugh.

"I'm serious," I tell her.

"Why?"

"Because sex has been clouding my judgment. Since you left, um…since we broke up, casual sex has been my drug of choice. It's been my way of pretending not to give a fuck. I told myself that my forty-eight-hour rule was because of my career, but it was just a front for not being able to handle emotional intimacy.

"We agree that we both made poor decisions after we split up. You married an asshole you didn't love, and I serial-dated to avoid love. I don't want to avoid it anymore. We're having a family celebration in the Hamptons this weekend, and I'd love for you to be here with me."

"I wish I could, Riley, but I have meetings scheduled. I've been throwing myself into work."

"It sounds like I need to get on your calendar then. How about this Tuesday, November the fourth?"

"That's our anniversary," she says, softening. But then her voice turns harsh again, and I know I deserve it. "Tell you what. I'll pencil you in. If you still want to see me that day, let me know."

"No, Ariela, you can write my name on your arm in glitter. It's a definite date."

She laughs, remembering how I did just that when we were making posters for Keatyn's student council campaign at the beginning of our junior year. It was sort of our first date.

"Mon-roar!" she says with a laugh, reminding me of Keatyn's campaign slogan. "Fine. It's a glitter confirmed date. I'm not sure about this whole celibacy thing though."

"Me either," I admit. "But I'm going to try."

"Look, Riley, I just have to know. Do you love Shelby or me?"

"You, Ariela. I've always loved you. The only reason I kept having sex with Shelby was in an attempt to keep you out of my heart, to keep from having it broken again. But, the truth is, it's still broken because it never really healed."

She sighs dreamily, and we say good-bye.

It's then that I hear the sounds of muffled laughter, and I see my brothers' heads pop up from behind the hedge.

"Celibate?" Braxton says. "What the fuck is that all about? Is that some trick I should try to get chicks to let their guard down?"

"Baby mama," Camden states.

"Wait, Ariela is pregnant with your baby?"

"You're out of the loop, bro," Camden says to Braxton before quickly giving him a rundown of my current life situation.

He takes the whole fucked up story in, and his first comment is, "In what world is celibacy *ever* the right answer?"

"Shut up, Brax," I say. "Actually, shouldn't you be inside, having some ice cream and then getting tucked into bed by Mommy?"

"Ah, fuck, man. Don't pull that big-brother shit. We're all adults."

"Go inside, Braxton," Camden says sternly.

Braxton looks defeated and does as he was told, but halfway back, he yells out, "I'm eating all the ice cream before you bitches get back!"

Camden and I laugh at him, but then Camden turns to me, looking serious.

I hold up a hand. "I don't need a lecture about my sex life, Cam. Just 'cause you and Annie have—"

"I wasn't going to give you a lecture. I can't believe I'm going to say this because I agree with Brax about celibacy never being the right answer. But I think, in this case, you do need to take sex out of the equation."

"Sex is always part of the equation," I say, chuckling, repeating advice he gave me when we were younger.

"What the fuck did I know?" he says, throwing up his hands. "I was, like, sixteen when I told you that."

"And I looked up to you."

"You shouldn't have," he says. "I didn't set a very good example. Now that I have sons of my own, I realize the last thing I want is for them to follow in my footsteps."

"Oh, now, don't say that. Pretty much all my partying skills as well as how to pick up a girl are thanks to you. Your boys will turn out fine. You have Annie to balance them out."

"So when you realized you liked Ariela, you said, *You're hot. Wanna fuck?*"

I run my hand across my face, my voice softening. "No, I didn't. Not with her."

"Then you need to stop following my stupid teen advice."

"Are you happy, being married?" I ask as we make our way back to the house. "Having kids? Being monogamous?"

"The answer to your question is no."

I look at him in shock. "To which one? Are you *cheating* on Annie?"

"To all of them," he states.

"You're not happy?" My heart drops for him, for all of them.

"No, I'm not *happy*, Riley. Happy is how you feel when you eat a snow cone on a hot summer day. I'm *more* than happy. I'm content and fulfilled. And every day when I look at my beautiful wife and my three chips-off-the-old-block, I wonder how a fuck-up like me got so lucky. But then I realize it wasn't really luck. When I saw what I wanted, what I knew in my heart was right, I didn't let anything get in my way. And I never will."

"If I remember right, Annie wasn't so sure." I chuckle.

"And who could blame her with my reputation? It meant that I had to work extra hard to not just convince her, but to also prove that I was the right man for her. And that doesn't stop when you get married, Riley. You have to keep proving it to the person you love. You can't coast through marriage or life."

"I've never coasted," I counter.

He narrows his eyes. "You've never coasted when you were passionate about something like your career. Speaking of that, can I borrow some money?"

I give him a playful shove in the shoulder. "Like you need it."

"You've outdone us all, little brother."

"Ain't nothing little 'bout a Johnson," I reply with a laugh.

"Gotta teach 'em young." He chuckles but then looks serious again. "My point is, if you are passionate about making things work with Ariela, I have no doubt in my mind that they will."

"I have a question then. And you have to promise not to laugh."

"Shoot."

"There's this house—"

He smiles. "Let me guess. Is it in Sonoma, near Keatyn and Aiden's place? I heard from Knox that he bought a place out there, too. That they are going to set up a studio."

"They are. The house I'm considering is big. Has lots of land. Do you think, if I bought it, you could help me convince Mom and Dad to come out once in a while? It only has five bedrooms, which would be great if I have kids, but Keatyn pointed out that it has enough land to build a few guesthouses."

"A West Coast Johnson family compound?" he asks. "Love the idea."

"You do?"

His acceptance almost brings tears to my eyes.

"Jeez," he says, slapping me on the back. "We had better get you back in the house and get you a drink before you start getting your period."

"Any suggestions on how to deal with the baby mama?"

"Yeah, stop fucking her. Get a paternity test. And remember, if the baby is yours, your relationship will be with the child. As long as you do that, Ariela won't have a problem."

"Are you sure?"

"That's what Annie told me," he says.

I smile. "Annie's always been smart."

"Of course she is. She married me."

SATURDAY, NOVEMBER 1ST
BAM'S CASTLE - TURIN, ITALY

Shelby

"OH MY GOD, I'm so hungover," Nina complains, glancing at me. "You and Juan shouldn't have left so early. You missed all the fun."

"I don't know about that. I'd venture to say, the reason we left early is so that *we* could have all the fun," I reply, causing her younger sister, Mia, to giggle.

"That's what happens when you can't handle your liquor," Mia chastises.

"Wait until you have five children under ten, and then we'll talk," Nina replies curtly, stopping short of baring her teeth.

"Give me a break, Nina," Mia says. "You have not one, but two nannies."

"That's simply due to the ages of the children. One nanny cannot care for children of different ages."

"That's funny. Most mothers manage to do just fine. You shouldn't be complaining. What you should be doing is volunteering at my shelter. Seeing what it's like in the real world. You act like you're some princess."

I study my soon-to-be family.

Juan is the oldest of the five. Next in line is Nina and her husband,

Louis, who have five girls; brothers, Marco and Mateo, and their respective wives, Julia and Rosa, who each have a boy and a girl; and then his youngest sister, Mia, a former model who is married to a very hot professional footballer named Gabriel, with whom she shares a two-year-old daughter. All four women will be standing up for me, wearing shades of gold and carrying blush floral bouquets.

"Look around you," Nina says. "We live in castles. We pretty much *are* royalty."

I burst out laughing. Because I could not hold it in. Any. Longer.

"What's so funny?" Nina bellows at me.

"She's laughing at you because you're being ridiculous," Mia says, giving Nina a glare.

I'm not sure what's going on between these two, but I'm thinking they don't get along. And if I had to guess, it's probably because Nina is not nearly as beautiful as Mia—or as sweet.

I don't reply. I don't have to because Julia and Rosa each pick a side, adding their two cents and causing a ruckus.

The French hairdresser who was flown in for the occasion twirls me toward the mirror and whispers in my ear, "What do you think, *mon chéri*?"

I try not to start crying. That's how beautiful I look. "You're a genius, Julian. Can I keep you?"

Julian gives me a grin and whispers, "I will leave a card." He clears his throat and glances toward the still arguing family. "For you alone. Call me anytime."

The wedding planner escorts all of us into a dressing room where our gowns are hanging on racks, steamed to perfection. The tailor helps me into my wedding dress and then secures the veil to my head.

The whole time, the sisters carry on. Even when Juan's mother joins us, they don't stop bickering. Compared to taking care of my addict mother, their petty spats don't bother me in the least. And, as Juan said last night, I won't have to spend that much time with them. Plus, he's the oldest, and based on what he said, he might possibly hold the family purse strings.

When Juan's mother presents me with a gift, I decide I've had it with their rudeness.

"That's enough." I don't scream. Or yell. I simply use a stern voice—the kind I used when some guy at the bar tried to put his hand on my ass. "Today is my wedding day. I won't have your arguing spoil it, so either get along, or please leave the room."

Nina curls her fists into tight balls, like she might take a swing at me. I give her the kind of smile you give to someone you feel sorry for.

I'm a little shocked when the bitch actually sits down, but then I realize she isn't just a bitch; she's a bully. And bullies always back down when they have been called out.

I turn back around to see Juan's mother smiling at me, still holding a gift in her outstretched arms.

"I'm sorry," I whisper to her. "It's just—"

"Your wedding day. You are quite justified. Now, on to something more pleasant. It is a tradition in my family to shower the bride with gifts on her wedding day."

"Should I open it now?"

When she nods, I take the damask box, undo the gold clasp, and find it filled with large strands of pale colored silk decorated with what may be real gold and precious jewels creating a delicate rope. All sorts of thoughts for how I could use this gift come to mind, specifically regarding Juan in the bedroom, but I'm a little perplexed as to why his mother would give me a gift with such an intention.

"This is *el lazo*, the wedding lasso rosary. During the marriage ceremony, it is placed around the bride's and groom's shoulders, forming the infinity symbol, to signify an infinite, everlasting union."

"That's such a beautiful custom." I turn my wrist over and show her my infinity symbol tattoo with the word *love* scrolling across one of the loops. "I love it. Thank you."

"Hopefully, it takes this time," Nina mutters.

"Nina!" Mia says, shoving her elbow into her older sister's side while their mother continues to ignore them.

"Juan's father and I have a gift for you as well. Would you mind if he joined us so that we could present it to you together?"

"I'd be honored," I say, feeling touched, as she wheels Juan's father in.

He takes my hand in his, so I sit in a chair next to him while his wife brings me a large velvet box.

Even though he looks like he could croak at any minute, when he speaks, his voice is deep and strong, "You are aware that our son was married once before. We confess to not supporting the marriage in our hearts. We felt our son was making a mistake when he married the first time. We want you to know that we do not feel the same way about your union.

"When Juan was but a boy of fifteen, we made a spectacular discovery in one of our South African mines—a very rare, vivid diamond called the Pink Star. While it was my desire to keep it as a gift for my firstborn's future wife, after the press got wind of it, we put it up for auction where it was sold for a record amount and brought much good publicity to our companies.

"It has never left my mind though, and when Juan told us of your engagement, I knew I must reacquire the gem. We sincerely hope you will someday present it to the wife of *your* firstborn son."

His mother then opens the box, and I stand there in stunned silence, my jaw practically on the floor. Lying delicately against the silk velvet is an intricate V-shaped diamond choker with more diamond clusters than I've ever seen in one place. At the point is the massive pear-shaped Pink Star diamond. Lying between the choker is a set of matching teardrop earrings, looking like they came from the Crown Jewels.

I try to speak, but no words come out. I just end up moving my mouth at them.

Juan's mother rubs her hand up my arm. "I know that *you* will appreciate the value and meaning of this gift."

"I will make Juan buy, um, some kind of vault, I guess. And we'll keep it in there, safe, until that time comes." I nod my head at her, tears filling my eyes. "I promise." I lean down to kiss Juan's father on the cheek as he gives my hand a squeeze. "Can you make sure it stays safe until we get back from our honeymoon?"

"Darling"—she chuckles—"we were hoping that *you* would start the tradition by wearing it today, on your wedding day."

"Are you freaking kidding me?" Nina exclaims, ripping the box from my hand. "This should be mine. She's not even related to us."

Her father gives her the kind of stink eye that makes her hand the box back to me.

"Girls, why don't you give Miss Benson and us a moment alone?" Juan's mother says.

Nina looks pissed but does as she was told. She's going to hate me even more now.

Once the girls leave the room, she continues. "There is a reason we felt comfortable gifting this to you. Do you know why that is?"

"Because my own parents aren't here. Because it's more than just a diamond to you. It's the start of a family tradition. The kind of tradition that, no matter the value, I never had. The kind of tradition I want for my child." I stare at the gift, transfixed. "And, because you know, above all else, I will respect your wishes."

When I look up and see tears shimmering in their eyes, I can't help it. I launch myself at them and give them sincere hugs.

"Will you allow me to put it on you?" his mother asks when I've finally stopped blubbering.

"Yes," I say with a grin as the makeup artist rushes in to fix my face.

"We have another gift. This one is from your groom. He said he tried to talk you into doing that newfangled *first-look* thing, but you wouldn't budge. I understand you don't want him to see you in your dress until you are walking down the aisle."

"Old-fashioned of me, I know. My bridesmaids were very vocal on that—well, all but Mia. She said she made Gabriel wait. I guess I just like traditions." I grin at her. "Not to mention, it's supposed to be bad luck."

"Mia was adamant about that tradition, and I suspect hers will be the only marriage that survives the test of time. Along with yours,"

Juan's mother says. "Now, let's see what your groom has chosen to give you."

She holds out another ornate velvet box.

"Um, I didn't get Juan anything. I feel really bad. It just all happened so quickly. One minute, we were out on his yacht, and the next, he proposed. And it's been a whirlwind here. What should I do?"

His mother gently places her hand across my belly. "You're already giving him the thing he desires above all else. A child."

"And you gave him the other thing he wanted. You are allowing him to continue his polo career. Actually, I know what I want to give him. It's something precious to me." I turn to a maid. "Where is my handbag?"

She quickly retrieves it, just as the wedding planner comes into the room and tells us it's nearly time. I dig to the bottom and take out the only thing I have left from my grandmother—a small catechism book, one she had when she was a child. I think of the jewels wrapped around my neck and dangling from my ears and realize that, to me, this book is equally as priceless.

"This was my grandmother's," I say, handing it to Juan's mother. "The only thing I have left from her. I've carried it with me everywhere since she passed."

"Let me take it to my son," Juan's father offers, the pink seeming to have returned to his cheeks. "I will tell him of its significance."

After he rolls out of the room, I open the box from Juan. Inside is something I did not expect—a rosary. Old and worn and looking just like the one I told him my grandmother used to have and that I always regretted not taking from my mother, who pawned it later. It wasn't worth much. I think she got all of twenty bucks for it, but I remembered my grandmother telling me that the colorful beads were semiprecious and that it was a gift from my grandfather on their wedding day.

Juan and I met at a hotel when he commented on my dessert. I ended up going back to his room. The next morning, as I lay in his arms, we talked. Not the typical morning-after crap about how you are going to call or how wonderful it was even if it wasn't. We *really* talked. Opened up our hearts to each other and spoke of our families. And I told him that losing my grandmother's rosary was one of my biggest regrets. He told me about his dreams, and in that moment, I think I fell in love with him. I just didn't think a guy like him would ever fall for a girl like me.

I WRAP THE rosary around my hand and take my place at the back of the church, waiting for my new family to begin the processional down the aisle. It's odd, standing here by myself. Part of me wishes Riley could be here to give me away. Seems odd since we slept together, but Riley is the reason I'm here.

When this is over, I need to tell him how grateful I am and how sorry I am for lying to him, but when the wedding planner nods that I'm up and I turn the corner and see Juan waiting for me at the altar, I'm not the least bit sorry about anything. Warped or not, it all led me down the path to the man I love.

And, when we say our vows and kiss, I know we'll be together forever.

JOHNSON HOME – THE HAMPTONS

VANESSA, THE GIRLS, and I arrived very early this morning, and they all promptly went back to bed.

I'm sitting in the kitchen, staring out the window, drinking a cup of coffee, and watching angry-looking waves roll into shore. The sky above is filled with menacing, dark clouds, and the wind has picked up, the sunrise barely visible. I open an app on my phone to check the weather, praying the storm will quickly blow through, so the kids aren't stuck inside all day.

"Heard you took my advice. But just to clarify, you were supposed to get back in the saddle again, not buy the whole damn horse," Camden says, cuffing my shoulder in greeting.

"What are you doing up so early?" I ask him.

"No freaking idea. Habit, I guess. I always get up early during the week to check the international markets. I was going to go for a morning run," he says, checking out the weather, "but probably gonna have to use the gym. Want to join me?"

"I think I'm going to skip my workout today," I tell him. "Relax."

"Been burning the candle at both ends? Working hard at Captive during the day and keeping the lady happy at night?"

"It's clear you're dying to talk about my sex life."

He pours himself a cup of coffee and then sits next to me with a grin on his face. "Hell, I'm just glad you finally have a sex life." He blows into the cup and then takes a careful sip. "You don't need to tell me about the sex—unless you're dying to brag—but I do want to hear about your new job and how it's all going. Are you as happy as you seem? Are the girls going to do okay in California?"

Even though my older brother can be brash and obnoxious in the way he goes about things, he really does care. And he was there for me when Whitney died even though he never wanted us together.

"We're all doing great. There is something on my mind though. I need your advice. It's about Riley."

"Business or women?"

"Baby mama. I think she's stringing him along. I don't think the baby is his."

"Why?"

"The ultrasound. Something about it looked off. I couldn't put my finger on it when he first showed me, but the paper wasn't right. Not like what they print from the machine. Do you think I should tell him? He was so excited about it, which shocked me."

"And you don't want to hurt him, right?" Camden asks.

"Right."

"Doesn't matter. You have to tell him. He needs to know now." A troubled look crosses his face. "Shit. I suppose I should take my own advice. Look, I have something I need to tell you. Something I should have told you years ago. I consider it my fault that you were even with Whitney, that you had to go through all that you did. I could have—"

I hold up my hand. "Stop. I know."

"You know what?"

"That Whitney used to send you naked pictures and flirt with you—practically stalk you—while she was dating me."

His eyes get huge. "Why didn't you tell me?"

"Why didn't you tell me?" I fire back.

He hangs his head and then looks out the window, lost in thought. "I wanted to, Dawes. I really did. But I didn't want to hurt you. You were in love with her."

"Do you think it's better for me to crush Riley now than let him be crushed later when the paternity test shows the truth?"

"She could change the paternity test, too. Maybe. I don't know." He shoves his hand through his hair, seemingly stressed. "Are you glad I didn't tell you, or did I completely screw up your life? Because that's how I feel. But the longer I went without telling you, the dirtier it all felt. I didn't want you to hate me."

"I'm glad you didn't tell me. At least in this case. I was young and in love, and I would have taken out my upset on you. She would have made it up to me somehow, promised it wouldn't happen again, and I would have believed her. It would have damaged our relationship, and that would have sucked."

He lets out a big breath of air, almost like he was holding it in for years.

"Hearing it from her and understanding her personality made it easier."

"I'm sorry," he says.

"It's okay. We were young and dumb." I laugh. "Might still be."

"Like Riley still is?" he asks.

I sigh. I understand what Camden went through back then. I also feel the need to confess something myself. "You're not the only one to possibly screw up at being a big brother. I may have recently given Riley some bad advice."

"What'd you tell him?" Camden asks, taking another sip of coffee.

"That he didn't have to decide between Ariela and the baby mama yet. That he could date them both."

"Ew." He grimaces. "I bet that didn't go over so well with Ariela."

"Ariela is married," I counter.

"But she's getting a divorce," he fires back. "Are you for her or against her?"

"You aren't around. You haven't seen how torn up he's been since she came back. The board wanted him fired after the whole Vegas debacle, and even Dallas wondered if they were right—if Riley did need a wake-up call."

"What stopped them from firing him?" he asks.

"*Keatyn,*" we say at the same time.

"You boys are up early," our mom says, joining us in the kitchen. "Thought I'd get up and pop the cinnamon rolls and potatoes in the oven. Are you going to work out?"

"No," Camden says. "I was going to run, but it's getting ready to rain."

"Can you keep an eye on these?" she asks, taking the rolls out of the refrigerator and placing them in the oven. "I'm going to walk on the treadmill."

After she leaves, Camden says to me, "Is Keatyn pro-Ariela, or did she just need a wedding planner?"

"I'd say Keatyn is fiercely pro-Riley."

"We should be, too," Camden says. "Don't tell him just yet. We had a good conversation about the situation, and I think his head is on straight—as long as he keeps his dick out of the equation." He rolls his eyes. "He told me Ariela wouldn't sleep with him unless they were monogamous. He's decided to be celibate instead."

"What? He's not going to be able to do that." I laugh.

"I don't know. When Riley puts his mind to something, he goes after it. And, like you said, it will keep his dick out of the equation. Normally, I would say that is a mistake—"

"Because sex is always part of the equation," I say with a laugh.

"I don't know why you two listened to me," Camden says, laughing, too. "We agree not to tell him unless he decides to marry her. It was one thing to let you marry Whitney; the baby was definitely yours. It's another to let him get trapped in a lie."

"DAWSON," MY FATHER says, "grab your coffee, and come sit outside to talk to your old man."

"Do I get to come?" Camden asks.

"No," Dad scoffs. "I see you all the time."

"Yeah, 'cause you're a lucky son of a bitch," Camden says with a laugh.

"Hey now, watch it. Your mother hears you say that, and you'll be in trouble." Dad laughs. "You're welcome to join us if you'd like, but we're going to have a very deep conversation about life and love."

"I'm out," Camden says. "Think I'll go wake up my bride."

"Means we won't see him for a while," Dad teases, then turns to me. "Let's make our escape."

I follow my dad out to the deck and look at the sky. "I thought it was going to rain all day, but it looks like the storm has broken up."

"Thank goodness. I don't know if I could handle everyone in the house at once. Speaking of houses—"

"The girls and I are moving in with Vanessa. That's why I wanted you to meet her. I'm in love with her, Dad, and I'm going to ask her to marry me."

"You are? When?"

"Well, honestly, when we first met, I invited her to come back here with me for Thanksgiving. Funny, but in the back of my mind, I knew then that I would propose to her. The plans changed with us here earlier, but I know it's right. Her father has given me his blessing and he's flying out here this morning. I want him to be a part of the proposal, too."

74

"Can I see the ring?" Dad asks.

"Oh. Well, no. I haven't gotten her one."

"Trust me, son. You propose to a woman in front of her father, you present a ring."

"Normally, I would agree with you, but Vanessa's ex-husband was very wealthy. He gave her the kind of jewelry you see on royalty. I can't compete with that." I tell him about the necklace I gave her that she wears every day. "While she appreciates the pieces that he bought her, she said that they were just things—that most were simply meant to impress, that they didn't have meaning. She's changed a lot, and she cares more about the sentimental value than the cost. That's why I haven't gotten one yet. I want us to choose it together."

My dad leans back in his chair. Usually, I know what he's thinking, if he agrees with me. But his expression is unreadable.

"I'm curious. Why the rush? Why are you moving in? Why are you proposing after knowing her for such a short time? What happens if it doesn't work out? You have to consider the girls in this equation."

"It will work out. Vanessa loves the girls, and they already love her. It's…I don't know, Dad. It's just right. But there's something else that I just found out this week," I say, my face lighting up.

My dad cocks his head and narrows his eyes, and I'm pretty sure he can tell by my expression what I'm going to say next.

"She's pregnant. We're having a baby."

"Wow. That was fast. You forget how to use a condom?"

"That's the crazy and amazing part of this. We didn't because she didn't think she could get pregnant." I tell him the story about how she miscarried, how her husband wasn't there for her, how the doctor told her she might never get pregnant again, how she thought she had cancer, and how she asked the doctor if it was a sick joke when he told her the news.

My dad is silent, which is unusual for him. His fingers form a steeple, and he rests his chin on it, seemingly deep in thought. "Sounds like it was meant to be. Congratulations, Dawson."

JOHNSON HOME – THE HAMPTONS

AT ELEVEN, EVERYONE—AND I mean, *everyone*—is present and ready to eat. Mom has brunch laid out on the big center island in the kitchen, and it's chaotic. Children are running everywhere. Boys are prevalent in the Johnson gene pool. Other than Dawson's girls, there are only two others in all sixteen of the second cousins.

I've been watching Vanessa to see if she can deal with it. It's a big family to spring on someone for the first time. Especially to someone who grew up with just her dad.

We're celebrating everything today. Four birthdays, a going-away party for Harlow and Ava, and an early Thanksgiving. This morning seems to be focused on the birthdays because Ava is handing out pointy paper hats, and Mom is bringing me a plate of waffles with candles stuck in them. Some things never change.

Everyone sings and eats. In what seems like two seconds, the food is gone, and the clan is outside, leaving the kitchen looking like a hurricane struck.

Vanessa and I do the dishes while Mom sits on a barstool—only because we made her.

"Now that you've met the family, what do you think?" I ask Vanessa.

"I see why Keatyn enjoys coming here. Always something going on. I heard all about the epic parties you used to have."

Mom raises an eyebrow at me.

"They were epic only because of the people we invited, Mom. Just like you always say, 'A party is only as good as the guest list.'"

"I like that," Vanessa says. "Keatyn always says something like that, too. About how it doesn't matter where you are for a holiday; what matters is who is at the table with you."

"Exactly," Mom agrees.

"But it is a little overwhelming. It's always been just me and my dad," she says, then turns to me. "I have a new respect for you, Riley. That you left all this to blaze your own trail in LA. I don't think I could have left. And, if I'm being honest, I sort of feel bad for making the girls leave all this love."

"Sometimes, you need a fresh start," Mom says. "The girls are very excited."

"I can't wait for them to see their rooms."

"Dawson says they are a little over the top, but I think that's okay," Mom says. "Speaking of my son, it's so wonderful to see him happy again. We have you to thank for that."

Vanessa catches Dawson's eye from across the room, and I notice him give her a wink. It's a simple, silly gesture, but based on the look of lust that crosses her face, it hits its mark. Dawson must sense this because he saunters toward her and holds out his hand.

"Would you like to go for a walk on the beach?" he asks her.

"NOW THAT IT'S just the two of us," my mom says, "tell me what happened at the fundraiser. I haven't wanted to ask because I know it's always a sore subject with Dawson. But I overheard Vanessa telling Annie that he told the truth about Whitney's depression and suicide. Is it true he's going to change the focus of the foundation?"

"Yes. Vanessa's mother passed away when she was young, and she only recently found out that it was suicide. Her father had kept it a secret all this time. She told Dawson it shouldn't be shoved under the rug and not spoken about. He took it to heart. You would have been so proud of him, Mom. His speech was so eloquent and heartfelt. And he read us the note she'd left him. He's kept it in his wallet all this time. Never told anyone about it."

"She left a note? What did it say?" Mom's eyes widen in surprise.

I can tell it's the first she's heard about it. I figured, if he had told anyone, it would have been her.

"Something about how suicide is selfish. How she was sorry, and he and the girls didn't deserve it. But that she thought they would be better off in the long run. It was actually a little more poetic than that, but you get the drift."

"What she did was selfish. What do you think of Vanessa—really?"

"I think she's good for him. And he's sure crazy about her."

Mom nods her head and then says, "Um, will you excuse me for a moment? I need to go have a word with your father."

A SHORT TIME later, I'm back in the kitchen, making myself a drink, when my dad yells at me to join him out front, which is a little odd. Usually, everyone congregates in the back.

When I get outside, I find all my uncles and male cousins over the age of eighteen, except for Dawson, waiting for me—and looking suspicious.

"What's going on? Someone getting a new car?" I ask.

"We're taking a vote," Uncle Charlie says. "About grandma's ring."

I roll my eyes. *Not this again.*

Grandma's ring is about the only thing this family ever fights about, which I find sort of funny. Although the ring is quite beautiful, it pales in comparison to the rock I hope to someday buy for Ariela.

I understand the sentimental appeal though. My grandparents did have an amazing love story. But I know everyone will vote how they always do. And whoever wants it will be told no.

But then my father and uncle speak passionately about their plan for the ring, and for the first time ever, I raise my hand in the air— along with everyone else.

JOHNSON HOME – THE HAMPTONS
Vanessa

OUR AFTERNOON IS spent poolside. Colorful, handmade felt banners hang across the deck, wishing the girls good luck at their new school. The girls are having a great time. Swimming in the heated pool, running around, and playing games. I have to admit, after the way I was treated by Bam's family, I was worried Dawson's family might not like me.

But they have been so incredibly warm and welcoming.

Ava runs up to me, soaking wet and shivering.

"Sweetheart, you need to either get back in the pool or put your cover-up on. You don't want to be sick your first week at your new school."

"I know," she says sweetly, taking the shirt from my hand and pulling it over her head. "I didn't want to get out of the pool, but Daddy is telling everyone to come into the pool house because he wants to make an announcement."

"Oh, I didn't hear that." I turn to Annie. "Did you?"

"No," she says innocently.

But I'm good at reading people, and I know she knows something.

"Does he have something special planned for the girls?" I ask Annie after Ava runs off.

She gives me a noncommittal shrug and then gets up. I follow her to the pool house and take a seat next to her.

"Oh, perfect. They're passing out champagne," Annie says, taking one off a tray, as Dawson moves to the front of the group.

"I'd like to make a toast," he says. "And I apologize in advance, as it will be a lengthy one. You all know that the girls and I have had a rough go of it the past few years. You've been encouraging and passionate about me moving past the tragedy and reclaiming my life. And, because of it, I finally went to California to work with Riley's company. I want to thank you for taking care of my girls and loving them while I figured out if it was the right thing for our family. And I can't tell you how much it means to me that you are all here, wishing us well with our move.

"I also want to thank you for welcoming Vanessa into our big, crazy family—and for not scaring her off. Because none of this would be happening without her. She's touched my heart in a way no one else could. She's helped me heal. Helped me want to live life again. And what I am about to do might seem crazy. Some might even say it's too soon. But I say, it's been a long time coming. Because what you maybe didn't know—unless you saw the last movie in the Keatyn Chronicles trilogy—is that Vanessa and I first met over ten years ago. We shared a drink. And we kissed."

I hold my hand up to my heart, thinking he's so sweet, but at the same time, I'm trying to figure out what he meant when he said he was going to do something crazy.

Is he going to tell the girls about the ponies I bought them?

Dawson continues speaking. "And it's a kiss from which I've never fully recovered. Vanessa, honey, will you stand up?"

He walks in front of me and holds out his hand. I put my hand in his and stand even though I'm not big on surprises—in business or in my personal life.

But with Dawson, I constantly find myself enjoying things I never did in the past.

He looks into my eyes and whispers, "Smile," as he drops down on one knee in front of me.

"Vanessa, fate brought you into my life years ago, and I let you go. This time, I'm smart enough not to let you get away. When Keatyn first introduced us, she told you that I was majoring in luxury marketing, and you said"—I mouth the words with him—"'What a coincidence. I'm majoring in luxury spending.' What neither of us understood at the time is that *love* is the ultimate luxury, and I want to wrap myself in our love and wear it forever." He holds up a ring box. "Vanessa, will you marry me?"

Out of the corner of my eye, I see Ava and Harlow jumping up and cheering. And, even though my head thinks this is too soon, my heart knows otherwise.

Tears build in my eyes as I smile at him and say, "Yes."

He opens the box to reveal a ring. One unlike any I've ever seen before.

"It's beautiful," I tell him, my eyes fixated on its vintage design.

"This ring was my grandmother's," he says, standing up and taking me into his arms. "It's always been a big argument in our family as to who should get Grandma's ring. This morning, over coffee, I told my father that I planned to propose today. Actually, remember when I invited you to spend Thanksgiving with my family, like, on our second date? I knew clear back then that I would propose to you in front of my family just like this. Anyway, after I told my dad, he sort of just left. I wasn't sure if he didn't like the idea of us getting married or what. But, a little while ago, he gave me the ring.

"I had heard the story about my grandparents' love, but I didn't equate them with mine until my dad reminded me. They'd met at a dance right before Grandpa went off to war. He never thought he'd see that girl again, never knew anything but her first name."

"*And that her lips were as soft as rose petals,*" the whole family chimes in, laughing.

"Three years later, he saw her walking down the street in New York, and this time, he wasn't going to let her get away. He asked her to go get a cup of coffee, and *the rest is history,*" the family says with him, causing me to laugh.

"You need to tell her the rest, Dawson," his uncle says.

"Let me," his father says, looking directly at me. "At that diner, he found out that she was widowed and had a two-year-old son—me. They were married three months later, and as you can see, they went on to have more children together."

Dawson smiles at me. Tears are falling down my face as he slides the ring on my finger and says, "There are three generations of Johnson love wrapped up in this ring, and I'm honored to be able to share that with you."

His family cheers and offers well wishes before finally drinking their champagne.

I give Dawson a big kiss. One that probably isn't appropriate for children of all ages, but I can't help it. I can't even believe that he just proposed. Part of me also can't believe I said yes.

"I can't wait to marry you," I whisper to him.

"If you're serious about that," his mother says from behind us, "why not do it here—today?"

I let go of Dawson and whip around, finding all the women in the family smiling at me.

"We maybe have been kinda planning all day for that contingency," Annie admits. "We have a truck full of flowers waiting outside."

"And everyone always talks about getting married in the gazebo overlooking the ocean," one of his aunts says, "but no one ever has."

"It would be fitting, don't you think?" another aunt offers. "Our parents built it in honor of their fiftieth wedding anniversary and renewed their vows there."

"And both passed shortly after," Dawson's mom adds solemnly. "We don't want you to think you have to. We can just decorate extra special for our early Thanksgiving dinner."

"And we bought everyone new outfits to wear in the family photos we planned to take tomorrow," another aunt says. "And we may have hired a photographer."

"Don't forget the band," Annie teases.

"Yes, well, they did meet at a dance," Dawson's mother rambles. "And every wedding—or Thanksgiving dinner, for that matter—needs a band for dancing afterward. I think it should become a family tradition in fact. We're not trying to force you into anything you don't want, dear."

I watch them all. How excited they are. I don't want to hurt their feelings, but…

"I would love more than anything to marry Dawson today, in front of you all, but I wouldn't feel right doing it unless my father walked me down the aisle. I'm sorry."

Dawson, who I almost forgot was still standing behind me, wraps his arms around my waist.

"Your father is here and watched the proposal. I could never ask for your hand in marriage without asking him first. I also knew you'd want him here for this. Turn around."

More tears fall through my lashes as I turn around and see my father standing there, Dawson's two little girls holding his hands.

"Yes, Dawson. A hundred times, yes."

SUNDAY, NOVEMBER 2ND
KEATYN & AIDEN'S HOME - CHELSEA

Keatyn

I GET A video call from Knox just as we're getting into a limo.

"What's up?" Knox asks as I answer. He's shirtless, in front of a blue ocean backdrop, and wearing the kind of goofy grin that makes me wonder if he's love-drunk or just drunk-drunk.

"Knox, you're on your honeymoon. Why are you calling me?" I tease.

"You're on *your* honeymoon. Why are you answering?" he fires back, causing me to laugh. "I'm calling because my love nest was discovered, and with the press release about the wedding going out today, it would have only gotten worse, so we checked out of the hotel. Speaking of that, Katie is going to be staying with me in London, and, uh, I am supposed to be staying with you."

"You're both welcome, Knox. Not that you'll see her much."

"I know, but she's excited to explore London. Says she can spend days at the museums. I don't think she will be bored."

"That's good because we'll be crazy busy. Is that why you called? Are you wanting to come here early?"

"Where is *here*? Are you in London or Paris?"

"We ended up staying in London. Aiden had some important

business meetings."

"Keatyn, we have a mere *seven* days before we have to be on set, and I plan on taking full advantage of those days. And, rather than mess with another media leak at a hotel, I figured, what the hell? I'm way too conservative with my money. I called Archie Barger. Rented his yacht."

"The tech billionaire?" I gasp excitedly even though it's just for show. I already know exactly where Knox is. "I've seen photos of it. And you can't call it a yacht. It's one of those super yachts."

"And it's totally and completely sick. When we got here last night, we both said, *This place deserves a party!*" Katie and Knox yell in unison.

I wave at Katie, who has appeared on the screen.

"Now, don't get me wrong, just because we're inviting friends doesn't mean that my bride and I won't sneak off for a quickie or even disappear for a whole evening, but still, it will be fun. Come on, sugar."

I roll my eyes. "Oh, boy, now you're sweet-talking me. Let me talk to Aiden. He—"

"We already talked to Aiden," Knox sasses. "He says he can take the week off. That, since you've been in London, he's been doing too much work. And it's *your* honeymoon, too. He shouldn't be working at all."

"You're right. Neither of us should be, but there's a lot going on with both of our businesses that sort of make it impossible. I'm assuming a super yacht has Wi-Fi?"

"Of course. Does that mean your answer is yes?" He waggles his eyebrows at me and grins. He loves getting his way.

"Yes, Knox. We'd love to come. Where is the boat docked?"

"Well, it *was* docked at the Marina di Portofino but is currently at sea, off the coast of Italy." He turns the camera away from his face and shows me an ocean panorama. "I'm not showing you any more," he says, coming back on-screen. "I want you to be surprised. Fly into Genova, and the yacht's helicopter will bring you out to us."

"Is the weather still warm?"

"Low seventies during the day, cooler at night. Absolutely beautiful."

"Who else is coming?"

"Well," he says, sighing dramatically, "I *invited* Dawson and Vanessa, but his girls start at their new school tomorrow, so they declined. Sucks. Because they got married this weekend. This could be their honeymoon, too."

"I'm sure they will go on a honeymoon later, once the girls get settled."

"Yeah, I know. It's the responsible thing to do. Right now, I'm all about the adventure. Maybe I'll retire, buy a yacht, become a captain."

"You can't retire yet, Knox. What about Riley? I thought he'd jump at the chance. He's always up for anything."

"Riley has a hot date with Ariela to celebrate—and this is so stupid—the anniversary of when they started dating in high school." He gives me an eye roll. "Why they want to remember that date, knowing all the shit they've put each other through since, I have no idea. They need to start living in the ever-fucking present, but whatever. If things go well on their date, he's going to bring her. If not, he might be here stag. Dallas, who is now my very best friend, and his lovely wife, RiAnne, are already on their way. Even though school is starting for their kids, too, that actually made it easier for them to get away."

"She's leaving the baby?" I ask, shock written all over my face. I can't imagine RiAnne leaving her three-week-old baby at home.

"No, of course not," Knox scoffs. "The baby is coming with them. There's a nursery with an attached nanny suite waiting for them. RiAnne is thrilled that she can relax, hang out with us, and still have the baby right here."

"A baby at your honeymoon," I say, shaking my head in disbelief. "Damn, Knox. Color me impressed."

"I know. Fuck. I'm getting old, aren't I?"

"You're maturing. Big difference."

"Speaking of babies, when do you think we will realistically be able to start filming *my* baby? And what about a release date? Have you been thinking about it at all? It's seriously on my mind all the time."

"What do you think I've been working on over my honeymoon? Dawson and Tyler are doing a great job of taking care of the day-to-day business, but this is different. This movie is *our* baby now. I've already had videoconferences with the Captive team about it. We have a budget and a time line. We just need to get all the key players in place."

"Seriously, I'm wiping tears from my eyes right now at your dedication to *our* baby."

"Knox, we're video-chatting. There are no tears. You're so full of shit." I can't help but laugh as he starts to allow himself to tear up on demand. "You'll be happy to hear that we have secured the costume designer I requested. And guess what?"

"What?" he asks, his face moving so close to the screen, all I can see is his eyes.

"Matt Moran is waiting to retire. Riley will direct, as planned, but he wants to help produce."

"Are you serious?" Knox's eyes get huge.

He pulls the camera back, and I can see how happy it makes him. We've worked with Matt for years. It's a good fit.

"We really are going to do it, aren't we, Keatyn? Win awards for this sucker."

"Is that your goal, Knox? Because it's not mine. You and I are personally investing a shit-ton of money in this film. First and foremost, we need it to be a box office success."

"Why can't it be both, sugar?" he says in that cocky Southern tone of his. "You're the one who spews out romantic possibilities. I've had box office success. I have a beautiful wife. All that's left on my bucket list is a family and an Academy Award."

"Just be patient, okay? If we're going for it—"

"Are we going for it? Because you're making me question your commitment right about now."

"Have I ever done anything small, Knox?" I ask, rolling my eyes at him.

"Hell no."

"That means, you can't pressure me on this part. You can't get all antsy and impatient. It's going to take some time to put together the perfect team."

"Like one full of award winners?"

"Actually, no. I didn't *ask* Matt to work on the project, Knox. I just gave him the script. Told him I valued his opinion and hoped he would give me some guidance on who to go after from a cast and crew standpoint. Seven and a half hours later, he called me, begging to be part of the team. And get this; all he wants is a quarter of a point because he's passionate about the project."

"That's encouraging."

I give him a sly grin. "Plus, he thinks it's his chance to win an Oscar, too. Crazy, with all his success, he's never even been nominated."

"How long are we talking?" he asks, already tapping his fingers on the counter.

"We have to factor in Captive's other projects, the fact that we have to build our studio space and sets from scratch, and of course, my pregnancy. The good news is, I'm pretty sure the set designer we want will be coming on board soon, meaning preproduction can start right after the first of the year. You'll be shooting *Daddy's Angel* from the time you are done with the *Trinity* location shoots until March—unless we decide to extend it another season. If we do, you'll be busy until June. The doctor says, if all goes well with my pregnancy, I'll make it to thirty-three weeks, which is mid-April. If it wasn't for the fact that we will practically be filming at our home, I wouldn't even consider starting until late fall, but I'm setting it up for July and August. We'll film almost entirely on set, and the location shoots will be within minutes from home. Postproduction can be done in about eight weeks. How do you feel about a Thanksgiving weekend release?"

"Are you serious? I love it!"

"It's bold though, Knox. And a big risk," I tell him. I'm really torn about what to do. "It's when the blockbusters release."

"It's also when moviegoers come out in droves," he counters.

"But it could backfire. The people who see movies that weekend sometimes only see one movie a year in theaters. They are like the people who only go to church on Easter. What if they want the blockbuster film and not ours?"

"They've been begging for a romance between us *forever!*" he cries out. "We'll finally give it to them."

"No, they will get it six months earlier when the last *Trinity* releases during Memorial Day weekend," I argue.

"No. They get a *happy for now,*" he says. "Not the big, sweeping happily ever after that we're going to give them in our movie."

"True. Are you saying we should go for it? A late-year release also has the added benefit of sticking in the minds of the Academy voters."

"I'm saying, when it comes to you and me, we should always go for it. Box office gold, sugar. And, by *gold*, in this case, I'm talking, pretty gold statues for everyone!" He punches his fist into the air like a champion, looks at me, and says, "Get your ass packed and on a plane."

"We're already packed and on our way to the airport, Knox," Aiden says, pulling the camera in front of his face.

"See you soon!" I yell as Aiden ends the call.

NEWS FLASH
Full Moon Madness?

Okay, people, things are getting a little weird. Maybe because it was Halloween weekend—the Day of the Dead, or whatever creepy holiday you choose to celebrate with floating pumpkins and skulls.

I'm going to start off with a warning because this column is as long and as tangled as the cobwebs you tried to decorate your front porch with.

For you skimmers, I'll start with the facts, then delve deeper into the details. There are official press announcements about all of these things, but I refuse to post them—mostly because they were about three weddings, none of which were mine. The press releases were all issued separately today, and although my depression went deeper with each announcement, it wasn't until the big one hit that I was officially done for. At first, it was no big deal. Just another announcement. Yay, someone got engaged. Cheers on your wedding.

You may think these things are unrelated, but trust me, they are not. They are like dominoes in a row. We pushed one, and the whole damn thing came tumbling down—along with my life.

Ladies, go grab a tissue. You're going to need it.

1. Knox Daniels, the sexiest man alive and my biggest celebrity crush, has left me devastated. I'm talking I'm lying-on-the-floor, dipping-Oreos-in-a-jar-of-peanut-butter, and sobbing-as-I-type devastated. Not only did he *not* marry his perfect match, Keatyn Douglas, he also *eloped* with a *teacher*. Yes. Let that sink in. A *teacher*. A normal girl. Why, Knox? Why? If you were going to marry a normal girl, I volunteered as tribute years ago.

2. Publicist to the stars, Vanessa Flanning, married Dawson Johnson, CEO of Captive Films, in a private ceremony at the family's Hamptons vacation home.

3. International polo star and billionaire industrial heir, Juan Fabio "Bam" Martinez married former cocktail waitress, Shelby Benson, in a private ceremony at his family's castle in Italy.

4. And, although this was just a tidbit in one of the press releases, it is important. If you wondered who planned the perfectly executed wedding for Keatyn Douglas, it was event planner Ariela Ross.

What is it with all these at-home, backyard weddings anyway?

Believe it or not, all these events are related. It's like playing Six Degrees of Kevin Bacon or something.

FIRST, WE LEARN that Knox Daniels was so distraught over Keatyn Douglas's wedding that he eloped just a week later in London with a *schoolteacher* from Cincinnati. Sounds like a prank or something, right? My immediate thought was that this was another Captive Films publicity stunt. Or maybe it was like those kids who send letters to celebrities, asking them to be their prom dates. Only she sent in a letter, asking Knox to marry her, and he did.

But, alas, there is more to the story. And I've got the scoop for you.

It seems the couple met at Keatyn's wedding just two weeks ago. Katie, the schoolteacher who was there with a plus-one, was introduced to Knox, and he was completely smitten. The two agreed to meet up the following weekend, but Knox showed up at the private school in Cincinnati where she teaches and had students help present her with a truckload of red roses. Knox then whisked her away to a luxurious penthouse suite in Washington DC where they toured the monuments like regular tourists.

We're told by Knox's camp that his new … bride—sorry, I can barely speak that word, let alone type it—is a big fan of the reality TV show *The Bachelor*—I mean, who isn't?—and that the roses, museum dates, and fantasy suite were all part of an elaborate bachelor-style weekend proposal. After begging Knox's personal assistant for more details and promising her my firstborn child—don't hold your breath, Missy—she spilled that Knox's engagement was completely over the top, first taking place on a yacht, which then turned into a version of a *Trinity* movie.

WE HAVE TO PAUSE HERE …

Remember the first time you saw Keatyn and Knox on-screen together? That magical moment where she had been kidnapped. She was tied to a chair, being taunted by Knox—who looked sexy as mothereffing hell, scar or no scar—when she challenged him to a fight. When he took off his shirt, it was like the sun opened up, and the heavens rained down singing angels. Although my favorite part was when Keatyn took off hers to "keep things fair." I swear, that is when Keatyn became my girl crush. Because 10 points for Gryffindor with that move.

Sorry, I'm now pulling up Internet photos of Knox's abs. Give me a minute.

Okay, sob, trip down memory lane is over. Moving on.

Back to the proposal.

APPARENTLY, KNOX GOT down on one knee. He proposed. She said yes. They kissed. And, when it came time to present her with a token of his love—I was hoping Missy would tell me it was a chip and meant the marriage wouldn't last long—he couldn't find the ring because it had been stolen by Dremel—the *Trinity* ultra-villain who never, ever dies even though Knox and Keatyn have killed him, like, what—five times now?

Anywho, this sent the couple on a movie-style engagement where they had to rescue the ring. Let's just say, our boy Knox did this engagement up big.

I was trying to do a little of the math. Private planes. Helicopter. Cast and crew. Location set. Stunt techs. Explosions. Penthouse suite. And the ring.

Knox's assistant wouldn't comment on the ring other than to say, "Much like the proposal, it is spectacular."

I'm ugly crying now.

Then it was off to London where the couple called in a favor with none other than *the* Prince of England—*the fun one*—to get the residency rule voided for them, so they could get a wedding license and be married at the Chelsea Register Office.

I have to say, this hurts me a little. Couldn't Knox have planned a fantastic star-studded wedding that we could have obsessed over? That I could have possibly been a guest at? Where I could have snuck in the groom's room when he was getting dressed and thrown myself at him for a possible quickie before he walked down the aisle?

Sorry.

So what is the Chelsea Register Office? It's the London equivalent of getting married by the justice of the peace at a courthouse near you. However humble it may be, I've learned that many celebrities have gotten married there in the past, including Judy Garland and numerous footballers, making it somewhat cooler—except that's not where they ended up getting married.

It seems that the Office recently stopped doing onsite weddings unless you want to go into a teeny interview room that only holds, like, three people.

But Knox and Katie had more people at their wedding. And this is where things get a little twisted. Standing up for the bride and groom were the honeymooners, Keatyn and Aiden Arrington—I'm told that Keatyn Douglas intends to change her name, even for movies, to Keatyn Arrington. What?! Say it isn't so. Keatyn, girl, if you are reading this, just say no. Don't give up the name you worked so hard for. (Although I would have been okay with you changing it to Keatyn Daniels. Hint, hint.) Because, remember, about half of all marriages end in divorce. I'm just saying ... —as well as Riley Johnson and Dallas McMahon, who flew to London straightaway. What you may not realize, if you haven't been paying close attention or are not a teen who has been obsessing over The Keatyn Chronicles, is that Keatyn, Aiden, Riley, Dallas, and Knox's new bride, Katie, all attended boarding school together—as did Keatyn's wedding planner, Ariela Ross.

Seriously, is this Eastbrooke place magical? My point is this: If you are one of my teen readers, get your damn admission application sent in, stat!

Let's pause the reunion part for just a moment and go back to the wedding. Get this; because the Office was unavailable, the prince, who I am told joined the crew the night before the wedding for a wild bachelor party—really, wild is that man's only speed—offered up, Kensington Palace. Yes, not only did this schoolteacher get my dream man, but she also married him AT. A. FREAKING. PALACE!

HOW DID THIS HAPPEN?!?!

Anyway, the wedding was lovely—yada, yada, yada—and the couple is off on their honeymoon somewhere on the Italian coast.

Okay, now ... after celebrating with Knox, Riley then flew home to the Hamptons where his brother, Dawson Johnson—another Eastbrooke Academy alum—proposed to and married Vanessa Flanning, who was Keatyn's high school BFF before she went off to boarding school.

Seriously, let's have a raise of hands here. How many of you are still friends with the people you went to high school with? I've eaten the last of the Oreos, and I am now sitting up and counting on my fingers. I have three, people. Three high school friends I'm still close to. And, by *close*, I mean, I see their social media posts, and sometimes, I like photos of their ugly babies. But whatever.

After licking out the peanut butter jar and threatening to open another bag, I call my teen niece who comes over to save me from eating my weight in Oreos. She sits on the floor next to me, sighs dreamily as she clasps her hand over her heart, and proceeds to quote the movie, telling me that Dawson and Vanessa first met at Keatyn's eighteenth birthday party.

She says—and I kid you not, this is her direct quote, told with nary a breath—"And so Keatyn walks up to Vanessa at the party and tells her she looks gorgeous and Vanessa sees Dawson for the first time and tells him he's gorgeous, too, which is funny because Gorgeous was always Keatyn's nickname for Dawson. Anyway, so Keatyn introduces them and says that Dawson is headed to NYU in the fall and plans to major in luxury marketing and Vanessa wraps her hand around his sexy biceps and, like, practically purrs that they have a lot in common because she plans to major in luxury spending. Isn't that the greatest line ever?

"And then she invites him to go get scotch with her. I can't believe they drank scotch in high school; have you ever tried it? I swear, it tastes like gasoline, and anyway, Dawson is just standing there, looking at her—at boarding school, Keatyn dated Dawson and told him about Vanessa because she was kind of a mean girl even though she really was a good friend to Keatyn, and Keatyn was just not confident enough yet to understand that—and he asks Vanessa if she's the alpha of all alphas, which is how Keatyn described her.

"I have to tell you that, even though Aiden totally has my heart, I did kind of swoon when Dawson called her Keatie, which was *so* adorable, and in case you don't get it, it's a combination of Keatyn and Cutie. But then Aiden called Keatyn *Boots*, which was even cooler, and ohmigod, did you hear she wore cowboy boots when they finally got married and that her dress had gold embroidery on it just like the dream and they had four-leaf clovers and cotton candy and he *bought* her a Ferris wheel?

"Anyway, it's really cool that Dawson and Vanessa have found their way back to each other, but what happened to Whitney? Dawson dated her before he dated Keatyn and was always in love with her and even broke Keatyn's fragile heart. I mean, sort of. Keatyn's heart hurt because, after the surfer, she was just afraid to give her heart to someone again, and when she finally gave it to Dawson—who gave her the most adorable key to his heart necklace even though she was actually in love with Aiden at the time but thought he wasn't in love with her—Whitney wanted him back.

"Although what happened after that was one of my favorite scenes in the whole movie—like, besides all the Aiden parts. Keatyn gets her heart broken because Whitney texted Dawson saying, *Baby, please come back to me*, and so Keatyn went to Riley—Dawson's little brother—and cried on him. Then Damian called—you know, *Twisted Dreams* Damian—and invited her to Miami, so she and Dallas and Riley flew there on this sweet private jet and they shot this awesome naughty video to make Dawson jealous and the crazy thing is that totally started Riley's career."

When she stopped to take a breath, I reminded her of her earlier question about Whitney.

We stopped to do a little research.

It turns out that Whitney and Dawson did get married, but she passed away a few years ago, leaving Dawson a widower and single father to their two daughters, who were recently accepted to a prestigious school just a short distance from Vanessa's grand Holmby Hills estate.

And get this; *that* is the estate Vanessa shared with her ex-husband, Juan Fabio "Bam" Martinez, who just announced his marriage to Shelby Benson, former cocktail waitress and the source of Riley Johnson's baby-mama drama.

If you saw the announcement and accompanying photo, you will have noticed that Shelby is sporting an engagement ring reportedly worth about twenty-five million dollars. I guess that comes with the territory when you marry a man who *literally* owns a gold mine. My sources also suggest that Miss Benson is with child—apparently, Bam's, thus the quickie wedding.

I told all this to my niece who summed it up better than I could have.

She's also brought me back to the living and gotten me off the floor and onto the couch with a bowl of some exotic recipe for hot buttered popcorn that has hot wing sauce mixed in it and is so delectable, I want to cry.

"Let me get this straight. Keatyn Douglas—who you wanted to marry Knox Daniels—married Aiden Arrington, causing a distraught Knox to elope with Katie Colter, Keatyn's friend from boarding school. Planning Keatyn's wedding was Ariela Ross, who also went to Eastbrooke along with Dallas McMahon and Riley Johnson, whose brother Dawson got engaged to Vanessa Flanning, who used to be married to Bam Martinez, who is now married to Dawson's brother Riley's former flame Shelby Benson."

I ADMIT, EVEN I had a hard time following along and mentioned it.

My niece gave me a stare-down and asked me one single question. "Have you ever actually seen The Keatyn Chronicles movies?"

To which, I had to reply, "No."

After being utterly appalled, she decides to rectify the situation, hits play on the first movie, and says we're having a movie marathon and watching all three.

Someone, please, I'm begging you, come rescue me.

The only good thing about all this is the popcorn, which she then proceeds to tell me is Aiden's recipe from the movie. And it's a completely horrifying but totally fitting end to this most devastating day in the history of my life.

P.S. I've never admitted to the fact that I haven't seen the trilogy in public before this. Please don't message me about it. I will ignore and delete that shit and probably block you for life.

P.P.S. *Well, shit, y'all.* Yes, I am now, in fact, talking like the adorable young Dallas McMahon, who grew up to be a partner in Captive Films, and I just realized that the woman he is married to and just had his fifth child with is RiAnne, Keatyn's and Vanessa's BFF. And that makes me feel all warm and fuzzy inside for some crazy reason. I also really wanna get high, but if I smoke with my niece, my sister will KILL me.

P.P.P.S. Eight hours and way too much popcorn, pizza, and full-sugar sodas later ... I want a boy to call me *Boots*, tell me we are *sort of like fate*, and ask me to marry him at the top of the Eiffel Tower at sunset.

Okay, okay. I get it now.

I am writing a heartfelt letter to Keatyn. I owe it to her. Here goes ...

Keatyn,

I am truly sorry for all the catty things I may have written about you and Aiden over the years. I think maybe it's because I was so in love with the chemistry you and Knox shared on-screen. Maybe it was the fact that I was in love with Knox, and if I couldn't have him, I thought you should.

I loved seeing how you and Knox met. How he was such a cocky jerk. And I loved seeing your friendship blossom.

I'm also going to say this: I was wrong.

You and Aiden belong together—4ever. And I wish you a lifetime of happiness.

(I might be writing this with tears streaming down my face. Because, the dirt, people. The dirt.)

Also, I actually just bought all the books because my niece said they were even better than the movies. If you want to go back and read K & A's love story, you totally should. (And, in a blatant and sadly unpaid plug, the first e-book, *Stalk Me*, is free. Get it now!)

#ifly #fourleafclovers #sortalikefate #boots #hottiegods #eastbrooke #truelove #wishonthemoon #sunsetselfie #thekeatynchronicles<3 #topoftheeiffeltowersunset #kcaddict4life

RILEY'S JET - EXECUTIVE AIRPORT

Dawson

"THAT WAS QUITE the weekend party," Riley says to the girls. "I bet you're excited to start at your new school tomorrow. Take a seat and get buckled up, so we can take off."

"Yay for Uncle Riley. Yay for plane rides. Yay for our new school! Yay for new ponies! Yay for new rooms!" Harlow cheers. "Yay for Daddy and Miss Vanessa getting married. Yay for our new baby sister, and yay for—"

"All right. We get it!" Ava says, annoyed. "Yay for everything! Please, stop talking. I can hear you through my headphones. And you know it could be a boy." She dramatically rolls her eyes and then puts her nose back up to her phone.

When both of the girls are situated, I lean toward Vanessa. "So what do you think? Boy or girl?"

"I'll be thrilled with either," she says, glancing down at her left hand. "I can't believe I went out to meet your parents, and I'm going home, married to you."

I bring it to my lips and kiss just below the ring she's wearing. "I can't either. But I couldn't be happier."

"Me either," she says, leaning her head on my shoulder.

I close my eyes and take it all in. I'm on my brother's jet, flying back to California, which is now our home. And I'm married to the woman of my dreams. I never imagined I could be so lucky.

When I open my eyes, I notice Ava is staring at us.

"What are we supposed to call her?" she asks.

"Call who?"

"Miss Vanessa. I mean, she's a *Mrs.* now, right?"

"What would you like to call me?" Vanessa asks gently.

"Well, Grandma and I talked about it," Ava says. "She said it's whatever I'm comfortable with but suggested either your first name—even though she thinks it's sorta disrespectful—or *Mom* or *Mama Vanessa.*"

Harlow, who I thought had fallen asleep already, suddenly opens her eyes and raises her hand in the air.

"What?" Ava asks her, rolling her eyes again.

"*I* talked to Grandpa about it," she says, pointing to her chest. "And he's older than Grandma and *way* wiser. He says we shouldn't call Miss Vanessa *Mama,* because our mama is in heaven, and that would be confusing. And Miss Vanessa isn't our mama. When she and Daddy got married, she became our stepmother. But I told Grandpa that I *won't* call her that because my friends will think she's evil, like in the fairy tales. Grandpa told me that *stepmom* is another word for *stepmother,* so I told him that I was going to call Miss Vanessa *Mom* for short." She turns from her sister and looks at Vanessa. "Is that okay with you?"

Vanessa tightly squeezes my hand, and I can tell she's fighting back tears.

"Yes, Harlow, that's fine with me."

"What about you, Ava?" I ask her.

She smooshes up her face in thought. "Do *you* think it would be disrespectful if I called her Vanessa?"

"Of course not," Vanessa answers for me. "You can call me whatever you'd like."

"As long as it's not late for dinner," I tease.

"Daddy, you're silly," she replies.

BEFORE WE'RE EVEN at cruising altitude, the girls are fast asleep.

"The Johnson family is known for their bashes," Riley says, getting up and making his way to the bar, "but I think this weekend will go down in the history books. Not only did we celebrate Halloween and October birthdays, we had a going-away party, Thanksgiving dinner, an engagement, and a wedding—complete with dancing. And learned we're adding another child to the brood."

"It was really fun," Vanessa says, leaning over and giving me a kiss.

"Our wedding was perfect."

"You sent a press release out today. What did it say?" Riley asks.

"I sent out three," Vanessa replies. "One announcing Ariela as Keatyn's official wedding planner. I mean, word had gotten out among the guests, but nothing had been stated publicly yet. Another about Knox and Katie eloping."

"What did ours say?" I ask her.

She takes the voice of a television journalist and says, *"Publicist to the stars, Vanessa Flanning married Dawson Johnson, CEO of Captive Films, in a private ceremony at the family's Hamptons home."*

"I like it," Riley says. He holds up a glass. "Anyone want anything?"

Vanessa undoes her seat belt, pulls her legs up on the couch, and then lays her head in my lap. "I'd love a nap. Pregnancy is zapping my energy."

"I'll have what you're having," I tell my brother as the flight attendant shoos him out of the way and makes our drinks.

He sits down across from me, and then he leans over and clinks my glass. "Here's to the Johnsons. Especially the one yet to be born."

BEFORE WE KNOW it, we're wheels down and pulling through the gates of our new home. Vanessa's driver drops us off in front of the house, and her butler, Bernard, is waiting at the front door.

I scoop Vanessa up and carry her over the threshold, causing the girls to giggle.

"The house looks so different!" Harlow screeches, running through each room. "I can run and not knock anything over!"

"You still shouldn't run in the house, Harlow," I tell her.

"It's really pretty. Way cooler than before," Ava states. Even though she said she's excited about everything, she looks a little nervous.

"Please leave your bags," Bernard says, "and I will take care of them. I'm sure Miss Ava and Miss Harlow are looking forward to seeing their rooms."

"Our rooms?" Ava says. "Are they different than the ones we slept in when we were here last?"

"Yes," I tell them. "The whole house got redone, including your rooms."

"Can we go see?" Harlow asks, zooming past us and toward the staircase.

"Yeah, can we?" Ava seconds.

"This is your home now," Vanessa says. "You can go anywhere you'd like. But your dad and I would like to show them to you."

We all go up the back staircase. The doors are shut, adding to the anticipation.

"I think it would be fun if we do this like we do at Christmas. We open one at a time, so you can see each other's room. Ava, is it okay if we go youngest to oldest this time?"

"Sure." She smiles.

"All right," Vanessa says, pointing to the correct door. "Why don't you do the honors?"

Ava opens the door, and Harlow rushes through it, only to stop dead in her tracks.

"Oh my gosh," she says, looking around. "It's a princess pony room!"

She rushes over and hugs my legs, then sets out to explore every nook and cranny.

"I have my own desk! And my own bathroom. And I have gold hearts in my bathroom! And I can pretend to have tea parties, and I can see the ponies from my window! And look! I can go straight from my room to the playroom without going out into the hall!"

"What do you think of your sister's room, Ava?" I ask, even though I can tell by the look on her face that she thinks it's great for her little sister but not for someone her age.

"It's perfect for her," she replies, nervously twisting her hair.

"While Harlow is busy, why don't we walk across the hall and take a peek at your room? See what you think."

"Okay, Dad."

"This time, I'll let Vanessa do the honors—"

"No! Daddy!" Harlow comes tearing out of her room. "That's

supposed to be my job! I wanna see sissy's room, too. Does it look like mine?"

"Do you think Ava would like a princess pony room?" I ask her.

She shakes her little head. "Nope. She likes boys now."

"Harlow!" Ava says in irritation as her sister flings open the door to Ava's sleepover room. "I do not."

"Wow!" Harlow says, taking in the room. "We can have sleepovers in here!"

"No," I say gently. "If you have sleepovers, you can have them in the playroom. This is for Ava to have her friends over."

"Which bed am I supposed to sleep in?" Ava asks, looking at the sets of bunk beds.

"Don't worry, Ava," Harlow says sweetly. "If you get scared, I will sleep in here with you."

"This isn't your bedroom, honey," Vanessa says, guiding her around the room. "This is your hangout space for when your friends come over."

"It's the coolest hangout space I've ever seen," Ava says, a smile playing on her face. "I love the funky chandeliers."

"Look, Ava!" Harlow yells, throwing herself onto the floor. "Furry sleeping bags!"

Vanessa takes Ava by the hand and moves her through the room, showing her the snack bar and shelves filled with games. "And this door takes you through to your new closet and bathroom."

"It's really big!"

"Well, a girl does need her clothes," Vanessa says. "And I can't wait to take you shopping. We can't have a closet like this only filled with school uniforms."

"And, look," I say, turning her around, "over here, you have a place to study and, over here, a place to watch television."

"And then there's your bedroom," Vanessa says, leading her into the next room.

Ava walks into the space and covers her face with her hands.

"What's wrong, honey?" I ask, rubbing her shoulder.

When she drops her hands to her sides, I can see that her eyes are full of tears.

"It's just all so beautiful," she blubbers. "I can't believe this is my room. Harlow and I have been sharing a room at Grandma and Grandpa's. Now, I'll have privacy. And it's a grown-up room. Not a kid's room."

"Well, you're not a kid anymore," Vanessa says, pulling her into her arms and petting the top of her hair. "You're a young woman. I'm so glad you like it."

"I don't just like it," she says, squeezing Vanessa. "I love it, Mom."

Tears immediately fill Vanessa's eyes and, well, mine too.

MONDAY, NOVEMBER 3RD
CAPTIVE FILMS - SANTA MONICA

Riley

"BABY MAMA, LINE one," Tyler says to me over the intercom.

I pick up the phone, already irritated. "Hey, Shelby. You back in town? I'd like to talk to you." I need to let her know how our relationship is going to change, going forward.

"Not exactly. Um, Riley, I actually have something I need—"

Tyler walks in and drops a newspaper article on my desk and mouthes, *Read this!*

Being that he never interrupts me on a call without good reason, I say, "Uh, hang on, Shelby. I need to put you on hold for just a second."

I read the headline.

International polo star and billionaire industrial heir, Juan Fabio "Bam" Martinez married former waitress, Shelby Benson, in a private ceremony at his family's castle in Italy.

"What the fuck is this?" I ask Tyler. "Why didn't you tell me about this? It was announced yesterday."

"Well, I didn't see it. I took the day off."

"And did what?"

"If you must know, Raul and I attended puppy power classes with

Cici."

"Who is Cici?"

He rolls his eyes. "Celine Elizabeth. Remember I told you we were expecting?"

"Oh, yeah. I do. Sorry."

He slides another long article across my desk. I read the title, and then my eyes scan down to what he has highlighted.

My sources also suggest that Miss Benson is with child—apparently, Bam's, thus the quickie wedding.

"The baby mama is now married to Vanessa's ex-husband, and they are expecting? Is this the same baby that's supposed to be yours?"

"The fuck?" I say. "Do you think she got pregnant by both of us?"

"You know, I have heard that's possible. Women have actually had two eggs fertilized by two different fathers. The babies come out like twins, but genetically, they aren't. It's quite fascinating. I think I read about it in one of the British tabloids."

I shake my head at him, leave Shelby on hold, hit another line, and call Vanessa. I hear her phone ringing just as she walks into my office with the same article in her hand and Dawson right behind her.

"Did you see this?" she screeches. "Bam is the baby's father, not you?"

"Tyler just showed me. And she's on line one."

"Well, before you pick up, look at this!" She flashes a photo of Shelby and Bam, looking happily married.

I hold my hand up. "Stay put. I'll get to the bottom of this." I take a calming breath and then pick the phone back up. "You still there, Shelby?"

"Yes. What I wanted to tell you, Riley, is that I got married this weekend. And I just had to call and thank you."

"You want to thank me?" I ask incredulously.

"Yes, if it wasn't for you, I never would have found the love of my life. You were nice to me when a lot of guys wouldn't have been, and I am ashamed to tell you this, but it isn't your baby, Riley."

"It's Bam's?"

"Um, yes. I'm sorry. I know I told you I hadn't slept with anyone else, but the ultrasound showed that I was further along than I'd thought."

"How far along are you?"

"I thought I was only eight weeks, but it turns out that I'm really twelve."

"That's a big difference, Shelby."

"I know, but the first month, I had a light period, so I didn't know until I missed the next one. And I had been with just you that month. The first time with Bam was, you know, just a thing, and then our paths crossed again at the hotel. I wouldn't have seen him again otherwise."

"I'm surprised he recognized you. You look different."

"That's just the thing," she says. "He didn't recognize me, but he was attracted to me again. That is just further proof that we were meant to be, you know? Please don't be mad at me, Riley. I was serious when I said I loved you. I just love Bam more. And, now, you can be with Ariela. I know you were confused about her, but you shouldn't be. I want you to be as deliriously happy as I am. And I'd like to pay you back for the clothes you bought me. For the bungalow."

"That's not necessary, Shelby. I wish you and Bam the best. Um, Shelby, I'm not sure if you are aware, but I know Bam. He was married to Vanessa, who is a good friend of mine. She does PR for Captive."

"I didn't know that. Small world, huh?"

"Did Bam tell you about her? About *why* they split?"

"He told me he made a lot of mistakes with her."

"Did he tell you those mistakes included a lot of infidelity?"

"Aw, Riley," she says, getting a little choked up. "Are you telling me that because you care? That's so sweet. I am well aware of my new husband's ways and fully support all his sexual desires. I'm really sorry, Riley. I did love you, but Juan is my soul mate. And he gave me this incredible ring that was a perfect fit, made just for me. We had an instant bond."

I'll bet you did.

"Well, that's fantastic," I say to her. *Fuck.* "I guess congratulations are in order."

"Thank you, Riley. Bam is having all my things packed up from the bungalow and shipped to us, so you won't have to worry about that."

"Okay, thanks. Bye, Shelby."

"Riley?" she whispers. "You are one of the most honest and kind men I've ever met. I hope you'll remember our time together fondly."

"Uh, sure," I say, hanging up and face-planting my head on the desk.

"What the fuck?" Vanessa says, exactly mimicking my thoughts. "Why were you being so nice to her? She lied to you, or she's lying to Bam. How far along is she?"

"She said that she's about twelve weeks. She was supposed to be eight weeks this week. Said something about a light period the first month, and she didn't know. That she didn't find out until the ultrasound."

"Do you believe her?"

"I do," Dawson says, interrupting.

"What? Why?" she asks, her head on a swivel.

"Because I knew there was something off about the ultrasound photo Riley showed me. It didn't look like the one you got at the doctor's office."

"Why didn't you say something?" I give him a hard stare, letting him know that I'm pissed.

"Because I wasn't sure. I figured, if she was lying about how far along she was, she'd show soon. Plus, you said you were going to get a paternity test in a few weeks."

I run my hands through my hair and then squeeze my head. "I don't even know what to say."

"Finish telling us what she said about Bam. How did they meet?" Tyler says, taking a seat, ready for the gossip. I'm surprised he didn't bring in popcorn.

"I'm not sure how they met the first time, but they became reacquainted at the hotel I put her up at."

Vanessa rolls her eyes. "Bam always gets a bungalow there. What else did she say?"

"She and Juan are *soul mates*, who are crazy in love. The baby was never mine. She was pregnant when we met. You all were right. She was a gold digger."

"And she literally just struck gold with Bam!" Tyler slaps his leg while bursting into laughter.

"Are you okay?" my brother asks, taking a seat in a chair directly in front of me.

I nod my head. "I think so, yes. I mean, this is good. I'm not the father. I don't have to deal with Shelby." I take a deep breath, knowing that I'm lying. I feel like I just got the wind knocked out of me.

"I'd bet money Bam isn't the father either," Vanessa goes on. "He's just a bigger catch. Did you notice, in the photo, she's wearing the ring he tried to give me? I wonder how many women he tried to give it to before one said yes."

"I don't know, but she said the incredible ring was a perfect fit and made just for her."

"Bullshit," Vanessa coughs, causing Tyler to laugh again.

"Well, Mrs. Johnson," my brother says in an irritated tone, "I hope that you couldn't care less about Bam or the ring."

"*Mrs. Johnson*," she says, practically melting and glancing affectionately down at the wedding ring on her finger.

"What I want to know is, why I wasn't invited to the wedding," Tyler chides Vanessa, taking the conversation in a completely different direction.

"Um," I say, getting up, "I need some air."

I STORM OUT of my office, go down the elevator, and bolt out the front door. I pace in front of the building for a bit and then sit down on a bench.

It's not my baby.

My heart sinks to the pit of my stomach. On one hand, I'm relieved, but on the other … I'm hurt.

I have my eyes shut and am trying to simply focus on breathing when my phone rings. I pull it out of my jacket pocket and see that it's Ariela.

When I answer and put the phone up to my ear, she doesn't even bother to say hello.

"Riley, when we spoke, did you know that Shelby was off in Italy, marrying someone else?"

"No. How did you find out?"

"Kyle has become obsessed with the gossip columns. You also didn't bother to tell me that your brother got married."

"It was a crazy weekend, Ariela," I say, getting pissed. "And I invited you to come join me, but you were too busy. Excuse me for not calling and giving you a play-by-play."

"Did you just find out?" she says with a sigh.

"Yeah. Look, I don't really feel like talking, Ariela." *Fuck. Why does everything have to be so fucking difficult?* "Today hasn't been the best day of my life."

"Does that mean you are upset Shelby got married to someone else?"

"Jesus, Ariela. I don't need this shit right now. Good-bye."

"Riley, no, wait. I'm sorry. Let me rephrase that. Tell me why you are upset."

"Why do you think? Because I had finally accepted the fact that I was the father. She showed me an ultrasound. A picture of my baby." I stop and take a breath, trying to keep my shit together. "Only to find out it wasn't ever mine."

"Hmm," she says. "You're not reacting the way I thought you would. I thought you'd be pissed for being lied to."

"I am, but I'm also really surprisingly sad."

"Oh, Riley. I'm sorry."

"Me, too. Hey, I'll talk to you later, okay?"

"Are you still coming up for our date tomorrow?"

"Yeah, sure," I say, not really caring right now.

IN THE CAR – HOLMBY HILLS
Vanessa

I CAN WEAVE a story with so many twists and turns that a journalist can't keep up. I'm able to spin just about anything, allowing my clients to stay a few steps ahead of the paparazzi. Right now, though, I feel like I'm in a tangled web of deceit.

I grab the diagram that maps out the school's pickup procedure and read it one more time. I've gone over every detail, but I still get an angry horn honk when I attempt to turn in the wrong direction. Fortunately, this happens before the children are released and I don't embarrass the girls.

Eventually, I find the correct lot, navigating myself through the cars parked in the pickup line.

With my job, I won't always be able to pick up the girls from school. I have an interview with a highly recommended part-time nanny later this week, but I wanted to be here today, when they walk out on their first day.

I glance around at the other people waiting. There's a mix of nannies, yoga-clothing-clad women, and those who are dressed more professionally, like I am. I wish RiAnne had stayed here to help me learn the ropes rather than leaving me to this fresh hell.

And I don't know why I'm nervous. Maybe nervous is the wrong word. I'm not nervous for me. I'm hoping that the girls had a great first day. I guess I'm nervous for them. Especially Ava. She was in the fourth grade at her old school—because she went to preschool an extra year— but due to her age and test scores, she was put in the fifth grade here. That's good because it means she and Fallon are in the same class.

Really, I don't know why I'm worrying. Yes, I do. Because I want them to be happy.

AVA COMES OUT of the school with RiAnne's daughter, Fallon, and another girl. They are a striking trio. All are tall with long hair—Ava's dark, Fallon's brown, and the other girl's blonde. I notice a lot of hair tossing and then giggles when some of the boys walk by. Honestly, Ava reminds me a lot of myself at her age. Smart. Confident. The difference is, I always felt like I had something to prove. Ava seems content in her own skin.

She makes eye contact with me. I start to move my hand to wave at her but quickly drop it to my side, not wanting to embarrass her.

Harlow, on the other hand, comes barreling out of the door with Carder and another boy in tow. She somehow spots me in the crowd and drags the boys over.

"Can Carder and Brady come over and play today? I told them we could swim or ride ponies!"

I wasn't expecting this, but it makes me smile. "It's okay with me if it's okay with their parents."

She gives me a hug, then takes the boys' hands and says, "Let's go ask!"

Ava slowly saunters over, eyeing her sister along the way. She rolls her eyes and says, "Figures she would have two boys holding her hands on the first day of school."

"Your sister is very outgoing." I get a shrug in reply. "Plus, it's easier when you're that age. They aren't thinking about boys in the same way as someone your age might."

She brightens. "I guess that's true."

"Did you have a good day?"

She opens her mouth to reply, but Harlow bounds back over.

She's frowning, and she has her arms crossed in front of her. "They say we have to set up a playdate in advance."

"We will do that then," I tell her. "What do you say we go home, have a snack, and take the ponies out for a ride?"

"I'm on a diet," Ava states.

"We'll be sure to make a healthy snack. And I know that my chef wants to talk to you both about your favorite meals, so he can put them on the menu."

"I want Chinese!" Harlow yells out, rubbing her belly.

As we're walking to the car, a woman passes by me and says, "Your girls are beautiful."

My initial reaction is to say they aren't mine, but I catch myself when I realize that they actually are now. And I hope that if their momma is watching over them, this makes her happy.

I give the woman a big smile and say, "Thank you."

ONCE HOME, THE girls open their backpacks, throw a mess of papers at me, and then run to change out of their uniforms. Harlow is back down first, fully dressed in riding gear. She grabs a carrot muffin and some actual carrots and takes off for the stable, not bothering to wait for anyone.

I call down to let the stable manager know she's on her way. I already had him saddle up the horses, just in case.

Ava, however, doesn't come down, and after about thirty minutes, I start to get worried. I go upstairs, knock on her door, and then gently open it, finding her sitting in one of the swinging chairs in her hangout room.

"Your sister already went to the stables. Are you not in the mood for that?"

I get another shrug.

"Tell me about it," I say, taking a seat in the other chair.

"I think I'm just jet-lagged," she says.

"You probably are. At home, it's nearly bedtime. Harlow interrupted us before we got to finish our conversation. How did your first day go? I saw you walking out with Fallon and another girl."

"Yeah, that is Fallon's best friend. Her name is Haley. She was nice to me when I visited, but I'm not too sure that she wants me around Fallon." Her eyes get misty. "I miss my best friend. I kind of want to go home."

"Was Haley mean to you?"

"No, she was nice—almost *too* nice."

I laugh. "You've gotta be careful of people who are too nice."

"I know, right?" she says. "Like, it seemed fishy to me. Like she's up to no good. And it doesn't help that she and Fallon are supposed to be best friends, but they both like the same boy named Keegan. And, when he sat next to me at lunch, I think it made them mad. But it wasn't my fault! The teacher made him."

"Why did she make him?"

"Because he and his friend were messing around in the lunch line. The teacher split them up. But it wasn't so bad because I couldn't sit by Fallon and Haley."

"Why not?"

She lets out a big sigh. "The whole lunch process is tricky, honestly, and something they didn't explain when I visited. When you go through the lunch line, you have to sit at the table in that order. Like, if you were behind me in line, we would have to sit next to each other. So it's important that when you leave class, you line up with your friends. I didn't know that, and Fallon and Haley didn't tell me, so I ended up at a different table."

"Did you talk to this boy?"

"Yeah, and he's so nice. I found out that he has horses, too. But they live at their ranch in Wyoming. He says he misses them."

"Did you invite him over to go riding?"

She lowers her head and nods. "I swear, I wasn't flirting with him. I was just being nice. Talking. But I think that I made Haley mad. That's when she started being really nice to me. And I don't know what to do."

"You can be friends with him. It's okay. And, if I were you, I'd probably text Fallon, like you usually do."

"I already did that. She wants to know everything we talked about, but I'm not sure if I should tell her everything because I think she'll just tell Haley. And he doesn't really like Haley. Says she's kinda mean." She lets out a dramatic sigh as she pushes her toes in the rug and then spins around in the chair. "The real problem is, what do I do about lunch tomorrow? He invited me to sit with him and his friend."

"Is that where you want to sit?"

"Yes."

"Then take him up on his offer."

"But if I don't sit with Fallon, she might get mad at me."

"It would have been nice if Fallon had told you how it worked and asked you to sit with them, don't you think?"

"Yeah, but if she had, I wouldn't have gotten to talk to him," she says, a happy smile spreading across her face. "But I'm worried, if I sit by him tomorrow, she will get mad."

"If she says something, just say that you sat with him because she didn't invite you."

"Oh, that's a good point," she says, giving me a hug. "You're good at this stuff."

"On that note," I say, "why don't you get dressed, and we'll go for a ride before dinner? You need to name your horse."

A SHORT TIME later, Ava is on the horse in full equestrian gear and looking much older than she is. She pulls out her phone to take a picture of herself on the horse, which she named Thunder.

"Do you want me to take a photo of you?" I ask her.

"No!" she says a little too quickly.

"She's Snapchatting," Harlow says. "When can I have a phone?"

"Are you supposed to be on Snapchat?" I ask her. "Did your father approve that?"

"Of course," she says, continuing to smile and snap away.

WHEN WE GET back from the stables, Dawson is just getting home, walking in the door and sliding off his tie. It's quite sexy. I mean, technically, we should be on our honeymoon.

I take a step toward him, but the girls are faster, calling out, "Daddy," and telling him all about school.

After patiently listening to everything that happened, he tells them to go up and get dressed for dinner. Then he takes my hand and leads me into our bedroom, where he shuts the door and immediately presses my back against it, giving me a hard kiss.

"How's my gorgeous wife?"

I bite my lip, afraid if I open it, everything will tumble out in one big jumble.

"What?" he says. "The girls look happy."

"It's just—no, you're right. They are happy. There are just a lot of moving parts."

He gives me a grin. "First days are always crazy, even without switching schools. Wait until they come home in tears."

I touch my hand to my heart. "I'm not sure I can take that."

"How are you feeling?" he asks, placing his hand across my belly.

"A little tired honestly."

"Hmm," he says, kissing down the V in my blouse. "I'd suggest a bottle of red and a roll in the hay with your new husband, but maybe we'll have to go with a cup of tea and a full-body massage instead."

"You've tried to massage all of me before," I tease.

"Well," he says, kissing me, "some of your parts are very distracting."

AFTER DINNER, WE watch a movie and then tuck the girls into bed.

When we retire to our room, I find a cup of tea at my bedside table with an envelope tucked under it. "What's this?"

"A wedding gift from my family. Open it," he says.

Inside is a brochure from an exclusive spa and resort down the coast in Mexico.

"Are we going on a honeymoon?"

He pulls me into his arms. "Yes, my parents are coming to stay here for the week, if that's okay with you. They'll watch the girls, so we can go on a proper honeymoon."

"Do you think we should go? I feel bad, leaving the girls when we just got here."

"Vanessa, your house is like its own resort. Everyone will have a great time. My dad can watch football down in the theater room and will be in heaven. And it will be warmer here than at home. I think we should take them up on it."

I look up into his dark eyes, meeting his gaze, and wrap my arms around his neck. "I think it's an amazing gift, Dawson."

"I have something for you, too. It's not really a wedding present per se. I had it planned before you said yes. I wanted to show you when we got home, and I was praying you wouldn't discover it on your own today, but things were crazy with the girls last night. I want this to be … special."

"Dawson, what did you do?"

"Why don't you come see?" He takes my hand and leads me out of our suite.

Nestled just off to the right is a room that was supposed to be my office, but it turned out to be too small and a little too close to the bedroom. I felt like I needed some mental and physical separation between the two, so I commandeered what were supposed to be two additional garage spaces to use instead. It also allowed me the ability to bring clients to my office without them having to come into the house.

Currently, the room is filled with racks of designer clothes that I wore when I was married to Bam.

He opens the door and flicks on the light then steps back to allow me to enter. When I hesitate, he gently guides me into the most perfect nursery I have ever seen.

"I didn't do a nursery last time," I say flatly, tears filling my eyes. "I was afraid I'd jinx my pregnancy."

"I know," he says softly.

I take in the details of the room. The wall behind the crib is covered in a tufted beige linen, making it feel like a cocoon. The crib is white oak and filled with linens in pastels—from the palest of blues to the softest of pinks. There's a beautiful silk Oriental rug in a deep brown sitting under a blue velvet sofa. Gold accents highlight a midcentury modern chandelier, the dresser's handle pulls, and numerous picture frames.

And the tall stuffed giraffe that decorated the playroom during my first pregnancy is holding court, seemingly overseeing the room.

"It's so beautiful and snuggly," I say, picking up a teeny white onesie draped over a brass ladder next to the changing table. "You did all this?"

"Well, technically, no. But I did tell Peyton that I wanted a room that felt cozy and calming. No bright colors. The playroom can be for that. I want this to be a soothing sanctuary. And we basically chose the color scheme to go with the giraffe. There's something about him," he says, walking up to the tall stuffed animal and petting his head, "that seems protective."

I walk over and pet the giraffe's nose. "He was the first thing I bought for the playroom. What's with the golden crown?"

"I snuck the girls in here this morning while you were getting ready. They decided to name the giraffe Princess Artemis Patches. But beware; now, they think they are so brilliant that they should be allowed to name the baby."

"It's actually a very interesting name. How did they come up with it?"

"Well, Ava did an Internet search and discovered that Artemis was the Greek goddess who protected the vulnerable. And Harlow liked Patches because of the giraffe's spots."

"Protects the vulnerable. That's so sweet. Thank you," I say, falling into his arms.

He tightly wraps them around me and just holds me.

A few moments later, he says, "Are you sure you're not upset? Our baby is going to be perfect. You got pregnant against all odds. I know everything will be okay this time."

Tears fill my eyes. It's not just the pregnancy hormones flowing through my body; it's because of this wonderful man who has flipped my life on its ass.

"It's the best gift I have ever received—well, besides you getting me pregnant, moving in with me, letting me be part of your girls' lives, marrying me, and most of all, loving me."

TUESDAY, NOVEMBER 4TH
ASHER VINEYARDS – SONOMA COUNTY

Riley

I PULL ONTO the vineyard property and see Logan's truck out in the field, so I park on the shoulder and hop out.

"How's it going?" I ask, greeting him with a warm handshake.

"Good. This is my favorite time of year. We're through with harvest, and all the wine is now fermenting in barrels—meaning Maggie and I are getting ready to take our vacation."

"Where are you going this year?"

"Thailand and Singapore. Some sightseeing and then some serious relaxing."

"You're both so adventurous in where you travel. I think it's awesome."

"Yeah, well, we decided kids aren't in the cards for us, so we're going to enjoy the fact that we can take off for a month without a care. Hey, speaking of kids and all that, what'd you ever decide about that house? We gonna be neighbors again?"

"I made them an offer this weekend," I admit.

"Before you found out about Shelby and the baby?"

"Yeah. It was good to spend time with my family in the Hamptons. I had a long talk with my parents, and they said they weren't opposed

118

to coming to stay out here. That's really all I needed to hear."

"Speaking of hearing things," he says, stopping to examine a vine. "I heard you're becoming a monk."

I roll my eyes. "You mean, the celibacy thing. That's the plan."

"I'm pretty sure hell just officially froze over." He shakes his head and chuckles.

We both turn around as we hear a vehicle heading our way. Grandpa Douglas stops the Gator and gets out. He's wearing overalls, a flannel shirt, cowboy boots, and a star-studded brown cowboy hat.

"Hollywood," he says, cuffing me on the shoulder and looking happy to see me. "Did you hear the news? I'm pitching a new reality TV show to Captive Films. It's called *The Celibate Life*."

He and Logan break out in a fit of laughter.

"Sex is like air," Logan agrees. "It's not important until you're not getting any!"

"All right, that's enough," I say, raising my hands in defeat.

"You know what they say, Hollywood," Grandpa says. "Having sex is like playing cards. If you don't have a good partner, you damn well better have a good hand."

"Thanks for your support," I say. "On that note, I think I'll head up to the winery."

"Aw, now, son, don't go pouting up to the women. Hey, heard through the grapevine—" He chuckles at himself. "Get it? That you made the Callahans a mighty generous offer on their house, contingent on getting your former flame's approval."

"What?" Logan says. "I thought you were doing it for you?"

"I am. I just wanted a woman's opinion." I roll my eyes. "You guys need to mind your own grapevines."

I give them a wave, get back in my car, and make my way to the winery, eager to see Ariela.

"WOW, YOU'VE SPRUCED up the place," I say when Maggie leads me up to Ariela's new office.

"It's coming along nicely," Ariela says, looking over her glasses at me.

She's sitting at her desk and her assistant—the ripped, handsome, young asshole—Kyle, is leaning over her shoulder, his body grazing against hers.

And I fucking hate it.

Behind me, I hear the sound of someone else coming up the stairs. I'm shocked to discover it's Ariela's mother.

"Mrs. Ross," I say, greeting her. "It's been a long time."

"Too long, son," she says warmly, gently patting my hand. "But I believe you'll be seeing a lot more of me in the future. My daughter has offered me a job, and I'll tell you all, I have decided to accept."

Ariela gets up and gives her mother a hug. "That's so wonderful, Mom."

"Hey, Kyle," I say, firmly shaking his hand when what I want to do is break it off his arm for touching my girl.

"Hey, man," he says coolly, like he hasn't a care in the world—least of all the fact that I want to whoop his ass.

"I was sent to inform you," her mother says to Ariela, "that you and Riley should head up to the guesthouse, pronto. Your lunch will be served shortly."

"Oh, okay." She steps back to her desk, grabs her cell, and then steps in front of me.

"Hey," I say, giving her an awkward hug.

She leads me down the stairs. We hop on a golf cart, and she drives.

"It's good to see you, Riley," she says, the wind blowing her hair back as she presses down on the gas pedal.

"You, too." *Why the fuck do I feel so awkward?*

"We might as well finish talking about it now, Riley," she says, cutting to the chase. "How are you feeling about everything?"

"I'm sorry if I was rude on the phone. Honestly, I was upset. Really upset," I say, my voice cracking.

She stops the cart even though we aren't there yet and turns to face me. "Because you cared for her?"

"No, because of the baby. Like, at first, when I found out she was pregnant, I was just trying to be a man and do the right thing. But I'll be honest. I wasn't happy about it."

I stop and push a strand of hair out of her face, tucking it behind her ear. Our gazes meet.

"Keep going, Riley. I need to understand how you are feeling. It's important."

"When we had the scare with her spotting and shit got real, I decided that it might not be as awful of news as I'd first thought. I was warming to the idea. But then, when she showed me her ultrasound, it was just so … unbelievable. It touched me"—I pat my chest—"deep down, and I suddenly realized that I wanted the baby."

She looks away from me and hits the gas pedal again, shooting us up the hill. She's quiet until we stop in front of the guesthouse, our lunch being laid out on the terrace.

I grab her shoulders and make her face me. "It's like I finally embraced it, only to find out it wasn't mine. She lied to me. And it hurts."

It's then that she finally hugs me. And this hug is tighter than usual.

I push her chin up with my finger and softly kiss her. "I have a favor."

"Since you're going celibate, I guess I can rule out the sexual kind."

I chuckle. "Yeah, probably. I still want you to go see the house with me. Today. After lunch."

"Fine," she agrees.

We sit down at the table and have a wonderful lunch, but the conversation between us feels stiff, and I'm not sure why.

WHEN WE GO to the house though, she sparks up. "Riley, it's beautiful. A little updating, and it would be amazing. Look at this view."

"Does that mean you like it?"

"Yeah, Riley, I do."

"Good," I say, letting out my breath. "'Cause I made them an offer this weekend that they couldn't refuse."

"So you didn't really need my input?" she says, sounding pissed.

"They said, if you hated it, they would let me out of the contract. Is it not the exact house we used to dream about?"

"It is, Riley." She softens. "But things were a lot simpler back then. Now, they are complicated."

"And I was thinking things just got a whole less complicated."

"I need to get back to work," she says.

I thank the Callahans for their hospitality and tell them we have a done deal.

"You want to tell me what's going on?" I ask Ariela as we're heading back out to the car. "Do you not want to be with me?"

"What?" She looks over at me in shock. "No, that's not it at all. Riley, serious question."

"Okay."

"Tell me again how you felt about the baby."

I put the car in drive and take off toward the vineyard. "Maybe, in a weird way, it was like a sign for me. Something I needed to prove to myself that I'm ready to settle down. To be a father. Since you left, I never thought it was in the cards for me, but the joy I felt was different. I just would have preferred that the person who was pregnant with my child was the person I loved."

"Do you still want kids?"

"Yes, that hasn't changed at all. In fact, I want them now more than ever. I just want them with you."

"Oh, Riley," she says, slumping against the seat. "I'm so relieved."

"Why are you relieved?" I search her face, trying to figure out why this is such a shock to her. We used to always talk about having children.

I pull into the vineyard and then drive up to her guesthouse.

When she gets out of the car, she pulls me inside and then searches the house to make sure no one is there.

"You're acting really odd, Ariela. Are you feeling okay?"

She doesn't reply, just throws her arms around me, her mouth finding mine. "I'm sorry I'm acting crazy. It's just that … well, Riley, I'm late."

I glance at my watch. "For what? I thought we had a date?"

"*Late*, Riley. As in my period is late. And, if I'm pregnant, the baby is definitely yours."

"What? Are you serious?"

"Yes. I'm actually a full week late, but I've been freaking out and too scared to take the test. I couldn't imagine you having two babies a few months apart with two different women. And I didn't know where we stood."

"Do you have a test? Like, here?"

"Are you kidding? I have, like, five of them. I keep buying them, planning to take them."

"Let's do it together."

"We already did that." With a sexy sway of her hips, she goes into her room with me hot on her tail. I can't wait to find out if she's pregnant with my baby.

She gets the tests out of the cabinet and spreads them across the bathroom counter. "Which one should I take?" she asks.

I check out all the labels, choosing a digital version and opening it. I read the instructions and tell her what to do.

When she's taken the test, she lays it on the counter.

We wait.

And wait.

"How much longer?" she asks.

"Two and a half more minutes. It's only been thirty seconds."

"Feels like way longer. What do you think, Riley? Is this something we should want? Or should we be praying it's not positive?"

"I think, whatever the outcome, it will be fine. If you're pregnant, we'll be thrilled. If you're not—"

"Is it bad that I kind of want to be?" she asks, staring at the stick.

I turn her around to face me. "Ariela, I love you."

She buries her face in my shirt. "I love you, too."

"If you're not, it's okay. It will happen for us when the time is right."

She lifts her head and nods. "I hope so."

Two and a half minutes later, we get the answer.

Not Pregnant.

Tears fall down her face the second she reads the results.

"I'm sorry I'm crying, Riley. I don't think this is the right time for us to have a baby. We need to get to know each other first. To date and stuff. But there is a big part of me that wants to have your baby more than anything. And that part is really disappointed."

"I would have been thrilled if you were, but it's okay that you're not. We need to take some time for us first. Really have some fun. What do you say?"

"I say that sounds good."

I raise my eyebrows and give her a smirk. "Maybe we should start now?"

"What are you suggesting? You've got that grin," she says, sliding her fingers across my lips. "The exact grin you used to give me to convince me to do something that could have gotten us expelled if we had been caught."

"And you were always glad you did it. Admit it."

She bites the edge of her lip, trying not to smile. "Maybe."

"That means, you have to say yes to this. Knox and Katie rented a super yacht, and they're off the coast of Italy. We got invited to join them."

"That sounds really fun, but I—"

"Nope," I say, holding one finger to her mouth to shush her. "No excuses. Maggie packed for you, and Kyle is going to take care of all your appointments. Those you can't miss, you can video conference from the boat. Come on, kitty. It's our anniversary. 'Bout time we do it up big."

She stands on her tiptoes and gives me a kiss. "Yeah, it is about time. Let's do it."

WEDNESDAY, NOVEMBER 5TH
YACHT - UNDISCLOSED LOCATION

Ariela

"IF YOU LOOK off to your left, you can see the Holy Grail," the helicopter pilot announces.

We left the States yesterday around two, flew all night in the luxury of Riley's private jet, and arrived in Italy this morning. If all goes well, we'll be having lunch with our friends shortly.

"Holy hell," Riley says. "Now, that is a yacht. How big is it?"

"One hundred sixty-eight meters," the pilot tells us.

"And is this all you do?"

"Yes, sir. I am on call twenty-four/seven. Would you like to hear more about this great boat?"

"Yes," I say. "It's obvious that it is a yacht, but all that stuff on the top almost reminds me of a Navy vessel."

"Privacy and security were of utmost importance when this yacht was designed. The foyer was set into the heart of the boat in order to divide owners, guests, and crew. While the decks are open air and allow for plenty of sunshine, the pool is built under cover for privacy. There are also below-the-waterline lights that can detect swimmers or divers in the area with motion detectors. The portholes are armored, and she is even equipped with flash light sensors and electronic countermeasures against digital photography. Although not yet installed, it is prepped for the installation of a missile warning system, and there is a small submarine on board that can dive, unnoticed, from the outside."

"Considering the tabloids are going crazy, wanting photos of Knox's and Keatyn's respective honeymoons, those features all sound awesome," Riley says.

As we move closer to the massive boat, I notice the *H* with a circle around it, indicating where the helicopter is supposed to land on the bow of the ship.

I clutch my stomach. "Are we really going to land this helicopter on that boat?"

"Yep! Isn't it exciting?" the pilot says. "I get the chills every time we approach."

He gets on his radio and calls the yacht's captain, letting him know that we will be landing soon.

"But the boat is moving—like, in the waves," I argue. "How does that work?"

"Wait and see," the pilot says confidently.

Riley looks over at me, a wide smile on his face. He grabs my hand and squeezes it.

I try to watch, but it makes me too nervous, so I close my eyes until we're on the ground—er, well, on the boat.

We're greeted by the captain, a steward takes our luggage, and we are escorted to the pool deck.

"You made it!" Keatyn says, giving me a hug in greeting. "Wasn't the helicopter landing on the boat a trip?"

"I'm not sure. I may have had my eyes closed," I admit.

"I did, too!" RiAnne says. "I had visions of a fiery crash."

"At least if you crash into the ocean there is plenty of water to douse the flames!" Dallas says with a lazy laugh.

I can tell he's a little buzzed already.

After we exchange hugs, Knox says, "Do you want the tour, or are you ready for lunch?"

Riley walks out onto the deck, drink already in hand, and says, "I think we're good here. How about lunch?"

"This yacht is amazing, Knox," I say. "How did you rent it?"

"With a whole lot of money." He chuckles. "Seriously, I've met the owner. We needed a place to hide out for the last week of our honeymoon, and a hotel wasn't going to work. I had Missy call him and see if it was available, and as luck had it, it was docked in Portofino. A quick trip, and we were here."

He pulls Katie onto his lap. I wasn't sure about the two of them together, but as she melts into his arms, their happiness is apparent.

Me, I'm still sort of in shock. First, because I'm not pregnant, and I'm upset about it. And, second, despite my best efforts on the flight here, Riley has upheld his celibacy pledge.

Thank goodness I didn't give up drinking. When the bartender offers to make me a cocktail, I definitely take him up on it.

It's amazing to me how, after more than ten years of no contact with these people, I feel more comfortable with them than I ever felt with the couples Collin and I hung out with. Maybe it's the fact that, although the setting is completely opulent and over the top, Knox didn't get this yacht to impress—which is the exact opposite of living with Collin. Knox simply needed somewhere private to finish his honeymoon.

"You're kind of a lucky bitch," I say to Katie.

"I'd say, we all are," Keatyn adds.

Riley slides his arm around my neck as he settles in next to me, and I can't help but think that Keatyn is right.

YACHT - UNDISCLOSED LOCATION
Riley

AFTER LUNCH, KNOX and Katie disappear to their stateroom for a *nap.*

I'm sitting on a couch near the pool, watching Ariela flit around in a barely-there bikini.

Dallas plops down next to me.

"You look stressed. What's up?"

"It's Ariela's damn bikini. How am I supposed to stay celibate when she's acting like a porn star?"

"What are you talking about? She's lying down sunbathing and not even moving."

"Oh, trust me, she's been moving. First, she prances out in that thing, leans over the couch, and gives me a sweet kiss. Which was fine, but then she walks out to the pool deck shaking her thong-clad ass. Then she does this slow-motion-stretch thing when the attendant handed her a towel. And I know she's trying to tempt me, because she cast me this sexy little smirk. Like I know you're drooling over my ass."

"Were you?"

"Fuck yeah. So then she leans over the back of the chaise and purposefully points her naked ass straight in my direction while she's staring at the ocean, letting the wind blow her hair all over the place. And if that's not bad enough, she did that thing—where she, like, fluffed her hair and made it look like sex hair."

"Sex hair?" Aiden asks, sitting down next to us.

"Where have you been?" I ask.

"Uh, Keatyn and I were, uh—"

"It's your honeymoon, dude," Dallas says with a smirk. "No explanation necessary. But it's cute how you came back out by yourself, so we wouldn't think you were off fucking. Where's Keatyn?"

"She's putting on her swimsuit. Where's RiAnne?"

"Down with the new rug rat. Riley and I were just discussing how Ariela has purposely allowed sweat to form on her upper lip in an attempt to seduce him out of celibacy."

Aiden laughs, but it catches in his breath when Keatyn walks out in her bikini. And she looks good in it. And I mean that in a purely platonic way. But any man, particularly one who is currently horny as fuck, looks twice whenever Keatyn walks into a room. This number is of the string variety, one that Keatyn always favors. Even though she hasn't been on a board since Brooklyn died, she's still a surfer girl at heart.

As Keatyn walks by, Dallas says, "Damn. Speaking of sex hair."

"Keatyn still doesn't look pregnant," I say, changing the subject because I already know Aiden will never kiss and tell. "Other than she looks like she had a boob job."

"Nah, I can tell," Aiden replies, studying his wife's body with a predatory grin. "Her hips are softer, but her stomach feels hard."

"I'm getting hard." Dallas lies back, laughing.

Keatyn takes a chaise next to Ariela. Ariela whispers something to Keatyn, causing them both to laugh, then she picks up her drink and takes a sip.

I nudge Dallas. "Look now. See how that drop of water dripped onto her chest. Notice how she hasn't wiped it off. She's just letting it sit there to torture me." I feel myself start to harden as I imagine my tongue in that exact spot. I shake my head, urging my dick to stop acting like a teenager.

"I think I need a drink," I say.

"I have something better," Dallas replies, pulling out a joint.

"Hell yeah," Aiden says with a grin. "Just don't let the smoke go in Keatyn's direction."

He lights the joint, and we puff and pass. I lean back, feeling relaxed.

Dallas requests a couple of bottles of champagne and whispers something to the waiter.

"Don't laugh," he says, "but I heard you were coming, so I baked a cake."

"I don't even know what that means. Are you referring to my birthday or to the fact that we're a little baked?"

"He means, he sent the crew out to get snacks," Aiden clarifies. "Remember what was always on hand at Stockton's?"

"I certainly do," I say. The nights we spent at our high school party place seep into my memory. There was alcohol, weed, dancing, and—

"Spicy Doritos, Chex Mix, sour cream and onion potato chips, Twizzlers, Atomic Fireballs, Reese's Pieces, Oreos, cheese and caramel popcorn, and pork rinds."

Aiden and Dallas both look at me like I've lost my mind.

"I can't believe you forgot the one you loved best," Aiden says, squinting his eyes at me.

"I swear," Dallas goes on, "every weekend, you sprayed it on her chest in pretty much the same spot that drop of water is on. I figured it would be the first thing to pop into your horny little mind."

"Oh God," I groan as the waiter sets out the junk food on the table in front of us. Then the sadistic bastard—probably on purpose—sets it down directly in front of me. "Cans of whipped cream."

Aiden takes off his shirt, grabs the bowl of chips that have always been Keatyn's favorite, and joins her in the sun at the same time RiAnne and baby Farryn make an appearance.

"Were you just propositioning my husband?" she asks. "'Cause, if so," she says, letting her eyes run down my chest, "Mama wants in on that."

"What the fuck?" Dallas says.

"Give me a break," she replies. "I'm just teasing. I can't drink, can't smoke. I have to have a *little* fun."

"How's my girl?" he asks sweetly, sliding his arm around RiAnne as she sits down.

I assume he's referring to the baby wrapped in her arms, but I realize that he's not when she says, "I'm good. Little Miss, here is fussy though. Thought I'd bring her up for some fresh air."

Aiden makes a beeline toward RiAnne. "Can I hold her?"

"Please," she says, handing the baby off. "God, those snacks look horribly disgusting. Those your choices?" she asks me.

I unscrew an Oreo and scrape the filling off with my teeth. "Uh, no. This was all your husband's doing."

"Look at Aiden," RiAnne says with a starry-eyed gaze. "He's such a natural with babies."

Aiden has the baby on his shoulder, gently patting her back, while he paces across the deck.

"Things sure have changed," I mutter.

"Not really," Dallas says. "We just have another mouth to feed."

"I meant, since high school."

"Well, I would hope so," RiAnne says. "We finally got smart and settled down."

"Now, now," I say, "I'm not sure *settled down* is the right phrase for it."

"Men," she says, shaking her head.

Aiden brings back a now screaming baby. RiAnne takes it out of his hands and proceeds to nurse the baby in front of me. I mean, she's got the baby, and her chest is discreetly covered, but I still know what's going on under there. And, for the first time, it doesn't freak me out.

"You act like settling down is a bad thing, Riley. What you haven't realized until recently is what you've been missing out on." She turns toward Aiden, who is sitting down across from us. "Right, Aiden?"

"Hey, don't drag me into this. I still don't feel like Keatyn and I have settled down yet."

"Yet, here you are, on your honeymoon. What's Keatyn's schedule looking like?" RiAnne asks. "I would think, with triplets, she'd be on bed rest at some point."

"She and Knox will wrap the *Trinity* film before the holidays then she's off until the babies are born."

"*Off?* As in not working at all?" RiAnne asks. "That doesn't sound like Keatyn."

"I mean, not under contract. Obviously, she has some projects she's working on at Captive."

"And I had a crazy dream the other night that I'm thinking of turning into a movie," Keatyn says from the sun deck.

"I didn't know that they could hear us," I whisper. "Shit, Dallas. I was just talking about how hot Ariela makes me."

"Women can hear everything," RiAnne says, giving me a smirk. "I think the baby's asleep. I'm going to take her back to the nanny."

When RiAnne gets up, so does Ariela. She stalks toward me, all bronzed legs and firm breasts. I prepare to pull her onto my lap and kiss her, but she goes into the pool instead.

"Fuck me," I whimper as she goes all the way down, getting her hair wet.

Dallas leans toward me. "Wasn't the whole celibacy thing really only in play if you were dating *both* Ariela and Shelby?"

"Um, maybe," I say as she comes back up, water glistening as it glides off her body. "Um, yes, actually. I think it was. No, it definitely was."

He slaps me on the back. "Go fuck that girl, son!"

"You sound like Grandpa Douglas." I laugh.

He giggles, too. "I know. I'm going to be a badass grandpa someday."

I get up and meet Ariela as she's coming out of the pool, possessively grabbing her and roughly kissing her.

"Fuck celibacy," I mutter.

"No, fuck me," she whispers in my ear, causing me to do what any horny red-blooded male would do. I pick up her hot thong-clad ass, throw her over my shoulder, and carry her straight to the bedroom.

Monday, December 8th
NEWS FLASH

Well, people, you're very lucky that I immerse myself in the celebrity world because I am the first to report about this simple little announcement that I found in an industry publication. I'll let you read it for yourself.

Captive Films announces Love Struck, *an epic romance featuring a man who gets hit by lightning and is sent spiraling through time. In each time period, he will search out his one true love. Leads will be played by Knox Daniels and Keatyn Arrington. Also attached to the project are directors Riley Johnson and Matt Moran. The film is set to release next year for the Thanksgiving weekend.*

HOLY SHIT, PEOPLE!

This is happening!

I'm breaking out the bubbly!

Here's my take on the matter. We all saw the photos last week of Knox Daniels and Keatyn—sorry-I-haven't-gotten-used-to-her-new-last-name—Arrington attending the *Trinity* wrap party. Keatyn looked gorgeous in a blue silk Valentino gown that showed off her growing baby bump. And, although Keatyn and Aiden aren't sharing when their triplets are due, experts say she's about four months along.

But I'm getting off track here.

We've heard rumors that, in the last *Trinity* movie, Knox and Keatyn finally get some well-deserved on-screen sexy times and that the film ends happily. But we all know that it's an action film. How happy can it be? Like, yay, we're all still alive!

Love Struck is going to be a ROMANCE!

And something they didn't mention in this little two-liner but that I have found out through my web of closely placed sources is, the script was written by Knox himself. Can you imagine? He and Keatyn have been playing love interests for over ten years, and now, finally, we will see them in the way we've all been dreaming of.

And get this; I was told that this movie is expected to be so epic that it might rival *Titanic* at the box office.

Tuesday, January 27th
NEWS FLASH

Now that the holidays are over and we're trying to sweat off those extra pounds we put on from all the cocktails we sucked down, the big talk in the movie industry is, for the most part, about who will win what award. The Oscar nominees were announced very early this morning.

And normally, this would be the big entertainment news of the day. Instead, the Internet is all abuzz over what I'm told is a spectacular sex tape. Okay, who am I kidding? I totally watched it.

And, if you haven't, my goodness, go do it now, girl.

Don't worry. I'll wait.

The subject of said tape is none other than Juan Fabio "Bam" Martinez and his former girlfriend, supermodel, Alexi Simpson. This tape apparently came as a big surprise to … well, everyone, particularly newlywed, Bam, who is supposedly trying to get it removed from the cybersphere. Of course, it's been shared and forwarded so many times, it's hard to tell where it even started.

The question I want to know is, why?

Why did Alexi release this tape now?

She broke up with Bam.

Bam is happily married and expecting his first child.

You all know how I am. I had to dig deeper. And that digging led me to Palm Beach, Florida—actually, I was already here, visiting my aunt—where polo season is in full swing.

And I do mean, swing. Wooh! The men here are so fine, I may never come home. Of course, my aunt reminded me that they are merely "seasonal" and will be gone before we know it. She also added that we should enjoy them while we can, but I am probably going to need therapy after that comment and refuse to discuss it further.

Although I may have taken things further with this patron. For those of you who don't speak polo, he's the rich dude who sponsors the team, and what really turned me on was watching him sabre a champagne. You can Google it if you've never seen it before. It was hot; let's just say that. Although I may have gotten glass shards in my drink. But whatever. #worthit

Anywho, I had to stomp on a lot of divots to get to this, but here's what I know.

I'm told by sources close to Alexi that, although she broke up with Bam, she was shocked and hurt by his royal wedding to the former cocktail waitress. Alexi was in Palm Beach because when she was with Bam, she supposedly developed a love for the game. But from the looks of it, I'd say she developed a love for polo players, as she has been working her way through the league—if you know what I mean.

Today, she was in rare form at the match and dressed to the nines. I have a love-hate relationship with that skinny, beautiful bitch.

Bam and Alexi first met at this event, so it's their anniversary of sorts. And I guess Alexi thought it was the perfect day to release a sex tape of them? As a sort of tribute to their past. I'm sorry, but I don't get it. I also think it reeks of jealousy and is just plain disrespectful to the woman who is pregnant with Bam's child.

Alexi has been blowing up social media today, saying that her phone was hacked and pretending to be *aghast* that it was released, but those who know her say it was totally premeditated.

It doesn't really matter though how social media savvy Alexi is, we're awarding the win to Bam's wife, Shelby, who was attending said polo event in support of her husband. (And looking fabulous in a Dolce and Gabbana ensemble. I swear, you can barely tell she's pregnant!)

When a reporter asked her what she thought of the sex tape of her husband and his former flame, she tossed her long tresses over her shoulder and simply replied, "I thought it was super hot."

Drops mic.

AND THIS IS why I am now enthralled and impressed with Shelby Martinez. She doesn't need a publicist. No damage control. No stupid Tweet war. No vague-booking. She shut down the drama with one single flippant comment. You go, girl.

Friday, April 24th
NEWS FLASH

It is with great happiness in my heart that I'm able to announce that Triplet Watch is now over. Aiden and Keatyn Arrington are proud parents. Here's the official announcement.

Keatyn Arrington safely delivered triplets, two boys and one girl, via C-section early this morning. Mother and babies are doing well. Keatyn and Aiden would like to thank everyone for all their prayers, love, and support.

First off, CONGRATULATIONS, KEATYN AND AIDEN! I'M

SO THRILLED FOR YOU!!!

Okay, now that I have gotten that out of my system, I can tell you more details about the birth. Although Keatyn has not posted on social media—and who can blame her?—her sexy-as-hell husband definitely has.

Can I swoon here, please? There is just something about a hot guy holding a baby, let alone three, that just sets my panties ablaze.

And Aiden, I swear, just keeps getting hotter. Not only that, but in honor of their babies' birth, Aiden will be personally donating a dollar for every bottle of Moon Wish wine sold in the next month, up to three million—a million for each baby. If there was ever a good reason to get drunk, people, this is it! You can say it's for charity!

Okay, back to the birth. Here's what I know.

Keatyn was on bed rest for the last four weeks. I'm told, the fact that she managed to make it to thirty-five weeks and five days with triplets is a big deal. When multiples are born early, they typically don't get to go home with their parents, instead staying in the NICU for weeks or even months. Aiden said in a social media post that, while the babies were immediately sent to the NICU for observation, the doctors were cautiously optimistic that they would only be there overnight.

And, now, drumroll, please. If you're like me, you are dying to know what they named their babies. Would they go in the direction of some celebrities and choose very unique, obscure names? Would they go in the direction of Aiden's sister, Peyton—who is married to Keatyn's childhood friend, Damian Moran—with ultra-cool rocker names like Cash, Jett, and Jagger?

It seems, instead, they went a more traditional and meaningful route, choosing family names.

Here are the babies' names, in order of birth:

Son: Asher Monroe Arrington
Daughter: Aubrey Lane Arrington
Son: Aspen Stevens Arrington

Let's take a moment to break these names down.

Asher Monroe is pretty easy. Asher is Aiden's middle name as well as the name for the very successful Asher winery. For those of you who have read or watched The Keatyn Chronicles, you know that Monroe is Abby Johnston's grandmother's maiden name and the name Keatyn was using as her surname when she and Aiden first met.

Aubrey Lane is a combination of Aiden's parents' names—Aubrey and Lane Arrington.

Aspen Stevens was a little trickier. The middle name, Stevens, is the last name of Keatyn's stepfather, Tommy, as well as her half-sisters, Avery, Emery, and Ivery. But I wasn't sure about Aspen. Turns out that Grandpa Douglas, the hilarious sage in The Keatyn Chronicles, is named Aspen Douglas. Aspen was also the middle name of Keatyn's late father, model, Mark Douglas.

So there you have it.

Keatyn, just wanna say that I'm wishing you and your babies the best!

<3

Tuesday, May 19th

NEWS FLASH

It's three in the morning, and I just got home from the *Trinity* movie premiere. I'm a little drunk, happily swinging my heels, as I sit down to write this.

So here's the thing, people. Mark your calendars right now. On Friday, May 22nd, there is only one place you want to be. That is with your ass in a seat at a movie theater near you.

And, when I say *ass*, I'm referring to the reason you want yours in a seat. Because Knox Daniels bares his ass in this movie, and that alone is worth the price of admission.

Let's just say that when his naked ass appeared on the screen, which was about four cocktails into the night, I nearly jumped out of my seat and yelled, "Stop. Rewind!"

Forget that it's Memorial Day weekend, and all your friends will be begging you to come to their boring barbecues. If you really want to have a hot weekend, head to the theaters. Sure, there is the requisite action film stuff in this movie—bad guys, bombs, national security threats, and amazing stunts. But I just have to say, there is a scene in this movie—spoiler alert—where Knox and Keatyn are in bed. And, let me tell you, they are GETTING IT ON!

And that deserves an IMAX-sized screen.

Anywho, in this scene, Keatyn has what has to be the most believable orgasm I have ever seen in a movie. Kudos to Keatyn for faking it really well—or to Knox for making it happen for real.

All I have to say is, LIFE MADE!

Keatyn, who literally gave birth to three little humans just three weeks ago, looked amazing at the premiere. She was wearing a gorgeous gold empire-waist gown that had all sorts of fringe and lace arranged in a beautiful way. I'm trying to remember the designer of the dress, but it is currently eluding me.

I can't even really tell you much about the after-party. All the stars were there—although they tend to stick together in those little roped off areas.

But Knox did come out to pee.

And I may or may not have stalked him.

And I may have actually spoken to him.

And quite possibly spilled a little of cocktail number five on his own *cock*-tail—as in the front of his pants. I was horrified, of course, but yet, not. Because, in my attempt to atone for my sin by wiping said spilled cocktail off the front of his pants with a napkin, I may have gotten down on my knees in front of him. And I may have used one hand to grab his ass in order to push him closer to said napkin.

And it may have looked bad.

And there may be pictures.

Actually, there are. My plus-one was snapping the fuck away, laughing hysterically.

I do have to say though, Knox took it all in stride. Once he recovered from the shock, he quickly snatched the napkin out of my hand and zipped into the restroom.

I tried to wait until he was finished, but my so-called friend—who is never coming to a party with me again—dragged me away from the area when a handful of ripped security dudes in suits arrived.

Hello, hotties.

Sorry. Where was I?

Yes. Smoking-hot scene. Smoking-hot movie. Go see it.

Must sleep now.

Tuesday, June 16th
NEWS FLASH

It's a miracle! After my alleged rubbing—I was trying to dry Knox's pants off, I swear!—of his privates at the *Trinity* movie premiere, I was a little nervous that I wouldn't get invited to anything Knox Daniels–related in the future. Like, ever.

So, lo and behold, I was thrilled when I received my invitation to an early viewing of *Daddy's Angel*, starring Jennifer Edwards, Knox Daniels, and Jake Worth. It's always interesting to me how the premieres vary by studio. Who's spending the cash freely—and by *freely*, I mean, the drinks at the after-party—and who's not.

Let's just say, while the *Trinity* premiere last month was a big-bucks release, the Captive Films party was completely over the top. Of course, there was the red carpet where I stood on my feet in high heels for four hours while all the stars arrived, hoping to get a single useful quote.

And it happened.

Knox recognized me in the crowd and said, "Security."

Actually, I jest.

He pointed me out, and I asked a brilliant question. One that every fan wants to know.

I said, "Any chance you're getting a divorce soon?"

He laughed good-heartedly, then gestured toward his gorgeous wife and said, "You think I'd leave this sexy thing?"

And, ladies, I know *sexy thing* sounds a little like something a '70s rock star might have used to seduce, and out of anyone else's mouth, I would have been like, *Ick*, but the way he said it was so adorable, I might have spontaneously orgasmed. Right there on the red carpet.

Let's talk about the movie. I mean, that was why we were all there. This movie is different. Something completely new to the industry. A new episode will release each week on the big screen. The thought of going to the theater for eight weeks in a row in order to see what may essentially be a television series seems like a big commitment, but Captive is also offering, through a paid subscription, the ability to watch last week's movie episode this week on your TV. If you're like me though, you are going to want to be at the theater. I just don't know if a small screen will do this justice. And you'd never get stars like this together on a television show. The commercials wouldn't pay enough to cover the costs.

If you ask me, the direct-to-consumer-distribution option is pretty freaking brilliant.

And the show.

Jennifer, playing Angel, easily morphs from her daddy's little angel to a promiscuous hellcat. And those scenes where she's getting down and dirty are with golden boy, Jake Worth, who plays the town bad boy, Jackson. I have to say, I love seeing Jake step out of the box to play this role. I was a little worried he couldn't pull it off, but, damn, does he look good in a leather jacket and no shirt. I'd be sneaking off to the abandoned railroad tracks and doing it in the dirt with him every day after school, too.

But shit gets real when Knox Daniels's character, Nathan, comes to town at the request of Angel's daddy to properly court her. I'm not sure yet, but I have a sneaking suspicion that Nathan isn't quite as good as he seems.

Can you imagine? Two bad boys after you? Angel is a lucky bitch, is what I'm saying.

Get your calendars out now and make a date with this hot cast.

NOW, WHAT YOU'VE been waiting for—details on the after-party. First off, the decor was gorgeous with a fire-and-ice theme. The best thing about this party—NO private VIP section. Keatyn, Aiden, Knox, Jake,

Jennifer—everyone involved in this groundbreaking project was out mingling with us normal people. And I spoke to them all.

And get this! Keatyn knows WHO I AM! She read my column—the slightly embarrassing one where I had a bit of a meltdown over Knox marrying the schoolteacher and admitted to never seeing or reading *The Keatyn Chronicles*. Anywho, she told me I'm witty and funny and that I have a great writing style.

And then she invited me to her house for a sleepover where we pinkie swore to be lifelong friends.

Okay, not quite.

But she did give my email to a very pregnant Vanessa Flanning, who is in charge of Captive Film's PR.

And guess what?

This was so exciting!

As Keatyn was handing the email I'd scribbled on a cocktail napkin—what is it with me and this group and cocktail napkins anyway?—to Vanessa, her freaking water broke! Turned out, her due date was next week. I can't believe she got all dressed up and went to a party.

Her hunky husband, Dawson, rushed her off to the hospital with my well wishes for a healthy baby.

EDITED TO ADD: Get this; I got notified by Dawson Johnson's personal assistant and told that after a very fast delivery—as in they barely made it to the hospital in time—Dawson and Vanessa Johnson welcomed a bouncing baby boy into their family at just after midnight on June 17th. He also mentioned something about replacing my shoes.

EDITED AGAIN TO ADD: The baby's name is Branson Johnson! Isn't that adorable?

Wednesday, November 18th
NEWS FLASH

This is pretty much the craziest thing I've ever heard.

After the whole water breaking on my pumps and me possibly stretching the truth about them being Prada instead of Jessica Simpson when they were replaced, I thought I had been blacklisted. Over the last two weeks, I kept waiting and waiting, wondering when and where the *Love Struck* movie premiere would be held.

And when would I get my precious invite?

But here's the deal.

There is *no* premiere.

What? No red carpet? No beautiful gowns? No wiping spilled drinks off Knox Daniels's junk? What's a girl to do on a Tuesday night in this town?

Also, where are the sexy trailers that leave us drooling and sharing them millions of times?

That's just it. Other than a few well-placed lightning bolt graphics in key demographic areas and a way too short but completely captivating *leaked* scene of Keatyn and Knox making out, there's been no marketing whatsoever for this premiere.

What is this voodoo magic?

As much as I love Knox and Keatyn, I fear that their pet project is going to fail.

BUT THIS AFTERNOON, I received a ticket, inviting me to come to a movie theater for a special showing of the movie.

Of course, I went.

I checked in, loaded up on free hot, buttered popcorn and Diet Coke, and made my way into the theater—but that's when things got crazy.

Standing just inside the theater were Knox and Keatyn. They were dressed casually—Knox in a pair of dark jeans that hugged his ass amazingly and some kind of shirt that needed to come off, and Keatyn in jeans, boots, and an adorable *Love Struck* T-shirt.

And they greeted *every* single person. I'm talking made eye contact, spoke to them, shook their hand, and passed out hugs. (I may have held onto Knox a tad too long, but whatever.)

It was the best premiere I'd ever been to, and I hadn't even seen the movie yet.

SO, LET'S TALK about the movie. Actually, I can't just talk about it. I'm going full-on rant here.

YOU WILL LAUGH. YOU WILL CRY. AND YOU WILL CRY SOME MORE. I'M TALKING UGLY CRYING, PEOPLE! The beauty of this film is undeniable, and I can see why they chose not to do some over-the-top party.

Because this film speaks for itself.

Can you say Oscar nominations for our favorite on-screen couple? And, Lordy, I'd thought the sex scenes in *Trinity* were hot. These were a whole other level. Because they weren't *just* hot. You could feel their love oozing off the screen during their most passionate moments. The sets were beautiful, the costumes lush. And the score will be playing on repeat in my home for the next two years.

After the movie finished, Keatyn and Knox spoke to everyone again as we filed out of the theater in awe. They thanked us all for coming and told us they secretly moved up the release date to this Friday. They handed out *Love Struck* T-shirts—just like the one Keatyn was wearing. And I may have gotten to hug Knox again. (I'm sure I had mascara all over my face after bawling my eyes out, but whatever.)

Now here's where things get really cool for—well, everyone.

Keatyn and Knox are going to be showing up at movie theaters across the country. Randomly. Can you imagine? You walk into your local theater, and there are Knox and Keatyn, waiting to greet you. To personally thank you for coming to see their film.

I know once word about this gets out, movie theaters will be packed.

As they should be.

Tuesday, January 26th
NEWS FLASH

It's that time of year again! Can you believe it's already been a year since we were last waiting for the Oscar nomination announcements? Where has the time gone?

And what a difference a year makes. I am not only awake, but I'm also fully made up and sitting in a conference room at five o'clock in the morning. Because I was one of the reporters who was invited!

As a child, I used to hold a microphone, look in the mirror, and practice saying, "I'd like to thank the Academy."

But, right now, I really *don't* want to thank the Academy.

Because who gets people up so fucking early?

I'm just here because I need to know if Knox and Keatyn's film—that I have now seen not one, not two, not three, but FOUR TIMES, PEOPLE!—will get any nominations.

I wait.

Not so patiently.

I'm given a cup of coffee.

It makes me jittery—and even more impatient.

All the boring awards are announced first. And I'm wondering why getting up so early is considered an honor. But as I look around at the well-known reporters sitting up straight and waiting on baited breath to report this news, I realize that I've officially made it.

Wait.

What was that they just said?

AND THE ANSWER is …

YES!!!

Love Struck has not only been box office gold, but it's also been nominated for EVERY major film award.

Congrats to my favorite on-screen couple! I can't wait to see you at the Oscars!

Now, I have to figure out how to get a ticket. Maybe I could be Knox's seat holder. Oh my goodness, I'm fanning myself as I have a flashback of Knox's naked seat—and by *seat*, I mean, his ass—in the movie. Because can you imagine being the holder of that? Maybe I should send the Academy a note, letting them know that since I've already held his, um, *cock*-tail, I'd be the perfect one for the job.

Or …

Sorry, caffeine has FINALLY kicked in.

I know what I need.

Captive Films, people. Are you reading this? If so, I am begging you. Can I pretty please with cotton candy on top of the Ferris wheel at sunset get an invite to your party?

I'll do anything!

(Within reason.)

(Sorta.)

SUNDAY, FEBRUARY 28TH
KEATYN & AIDEN'S BEACH HOUSE - MALIBU

Keatyn

I FEED THE babies and then get them tucked in and back to sleep as the dawn begins to light the night sky. The babies are ten months old and finally sleeping through most of the night. They were small when they were born, as to be expected with triplets, but are pretty well caught up now.

Asher and Aubrey are all sprawled out in their cribs. Even in their sleep, they remind me of Aiden. Aspen sleeps more like me, all curled up into a ball. At this age, they are starting to have their own little personalities, which makes it so much fun. All three are babbling. Asher, the oldest by a few minutes, is already saying a few words and seems eager to converse with anyone who will listen. Aubrey and Aspen seem content with babbling to each other. Aiden thinks that Aspen will be the athlete of the three. While the other two are happy with crawling everywhere, he's already an expert at cruising—pulling himself up to standing and then using furniture to help him get around. I don't know for sure if it shows athletic ability or just that he's willing to try anything first, to forge his own path.

I close my eyes and soak up the silence, that wonderful sound of your sweet, content babies sleeping.

I love getting up in the morning with them and having that time when nothing else is happening in life. Normally, I go back to bed and snuggle up with Aiden, but this morning, as I move through the house, I stop to look out the window at the ocean.

And maybe it's because of what day it is. Or maybe because it's been a while. But I feel the ocean calling to me.

I quietly sneak back into the bedroom, grab a bikini, throw it on, and then make my way out to the garage. My dry suit is hanging in its usual spot, my board waiting for my return.

I remember how I thought I was going to pass out when Brooklyn surprised me with the hot-pink-and-orange custom graphics surfboard for my sixteenth birthday. My hand flits across the rail to the *Life Is Divine Chaos* sticker he added before he left to go on the pro tour. I spend a lot of time waxing the board, doing it exactly how Brooklyn taught me, then put the dry suit halfway on, leaving my upper body exposed to the elements, and make my way down to the sand.

Before Brooklyn would go out to compete, he used to kiss the *Chaos* tattoo on his wrist for luck. I kiss my finger and then reach down and press it against the *Chaos* tattoo on my hip. I zip up my suit and go out into the water.

The light hits the water, causing it to sparkle. The sun feels warm on my face. It feels good to be on a board again. I close my eyes and remember him. A montage of our life together—from the day I met him when he taught me how to surf to the day I heard he'd died.

Tears roll down my face as I look up to the sky and ask him why for the millionth time. *Why was he surfing in a storm? Why did he have to be so reckless with his life?*

I'm sitting on my surfboard, just letting the waves push it to shore, and then swimming back out. I've yet to get up on it. For some reason, none of the waves feel right. Maybe I shouldn't even be out in the water or on a surfboard today of all days.

And it doesn't help that the Academy Awards are tonight. Or that Captive Films' *Love Struck* was nominated for so many awards. I fought with Dallas and Riley to keep the name when we sold the company, but it was worth every penny.

I'll never forget the day, when our ordeal with the stalker was over and we were finally back together on our beach.

"I think the new name should remind us of this, Brooklyn. Of all we went through. Of how we've both changed. I don't ever want to lose sight of what's important in life again."

B reaches in his pocket and pulls out a joint. "Haven't had one of these in a while. What do you think?"

"I think I love you."

"I love you, too." He lights up, takes a few puffs, and passes it to me.

"Ah," I say, relaxing completely.

We don't say anything.

Just smoke in a comfortable silence.

"Captive Films," he finally says.

"Captive?"

"Yeah. Vincent held our lives captive."

"And we wanna hold our audiences captive."

He grins. "Exactly."

"That's perfect. You cool with having that name on your surfboard?"

"I'd be honored."

I open my eyes and look down at my board. Opposite the *Life Is Divine Chaos* sticker is the one with the Captive Films logo.

Brooklyn is getting ready to start his second year on tour. All our friends are coming over to hang out all day, but it's just me, Aiden, Damian, and Brooklyn who got up early to surf. We've got our boards in the sand, waiting for the sun to come up, when B runs his hand across our boards.

"Something's missing," he says.

I look closely at my board, checking that it's properly waxed.

"It looks good to me," Aiden says.

"So does mine," Damian agrees.

Brooklyn pulls three stickers out from behind his back and carefully places them on each one of our boards. "Just because you're not going with me doesn't mean we're not all on the same team," he says.

Brooklyn wouldn't want me to be out here, crying. He'd tell me it was a waste of good waves, but I can't stop the tears. Through the haze, I see Aiden on a board, swimming out toward me.

"What are you doing out here? You haven't surfed since ... Brooklyn."

"You know what today is, right?"

"The Academy Awards, of course."

"And *February the twenty-eighth*. The day B died."

He sucks in a breath of air. "I didn't realize. Things have been so busy with the babies and with your nomination."

"I still miss him, Aiden."

"I can tell you've been crying," he says, gently brushing his finger across my cheek. "He'd be proud of you. Especially today."

"I'm not sure about that. I'm really nervous, and he'd probably tell me I just needed to chill and let fate figure it all out. But I wish I could just make it happen. I really want Knox to win Best Actor. And I really want Riley to get Director or Best Picture."

"And what about you?" he asks, gliding his hand down to my shoulder.

"I'm not going to win, Aiden. The other nominees ... well, you saw the list. Half of them are my idols, and the others have all won before."

He leans across his board and kisses me, causing warmth to spread throughout my body—the fire that is and has always been Aiden heating me up.

"Your mom called this morning. Apparently, the whole family is coming to the Captive Films watch party. They're even making Lincoln join in the fun. Can you even imagine how bored the kid will be? But they all want to celebrate with you regardless of the outcome."

"Aiden, please. I came out here because I *don't* want to think about it. It's all anyone has talked about since they announced the nominees."

He nods and then takes my hand.

I breathe in the cool, salty air and relax.

After a few moments, I start to feel the waves building underneath me. I drop Aiden's hand, flip my board around, and paddle out, sensing the right moment—feeling the wave gathering strength, knowing it will be the perfect one.

Then I do it. For the first time since Brooklyn died, I get up on my board. I feel like I become one with the ocean as a combination of weightlessness and power fills me. Time ceases to exist, but at the same time, I know that I'm exactly where I'm supposed to be.

"Life is divine chaos, Keats. It's messy, and it's supposed to be that way."

When I get to shore, emotion overcomes me, and I clutch my chest as I look up at the cloudless sky above me.

Memories flash through my head. Brooklyn saying I was a natural. Vincent dying in my arms.

"My grandmother would be proud I met the girl I'm going to make a star here, on her beach."

As the chaos inside me threatens, I turn around and watch Aiden catch a wave. He rides it to shore, drops his board in the sand, and then pulls me into his arms.

A godly smile spreads across his face. "You looked good out there."

"It felt good. I also realized that what I told you was the truth. I don't care if I win. I thought maybe I was just subconsciously telling myself that, so I wouldn't get my hopes up. Especially after Vanessa sent me the Vegas odds. I'm a long shot. But being out there, I realized that none of it matters."

"Regardless of what Vegas thinks, I'd still take the bet," he says, raising an eyebrow at me in challenge.

I cock my head. "Oh, really?"

"Yes. The question is, what do I get if you win?"

"Aiden, seriously, it's not going to happen. Sure, Knox and I won the People's Choice Awards for best actor and actress, but we always do. I don't need an award to prove my success. I'm just thrilled—"

"To have been nominated," he says, kissing me. "Give me a fucking break."

"Aiden! But it's the truth. I would much rather it be a commercial success. I already financially bet on the movie, and we're all definitely reaping the rewards."

Aiden spins me out of his arms in a silly dance move. "That's the answer then."

I squint my eyes at him. "What's the answer?"

"What I get if you win." He pulls me back close.

I kiss down his neck, breathing him in. "What could you possibly want, Aiden? We have each other and three beautiful babies."

He pushes my chin up so that I have to gaze into his gorgeous green eyes. "Who will be celebrating their first birthday in a few months." He gives me his grin and raises his eyebrows. "We always said we wanted at least four children."

"Yes, well, that was before we got three babies at once. Are you saying that's what you want? That, if I win an Oscar, we have another baby?"

"That's exactly what I'm saying." His eyes sparkle. "You'd better plan your speech because, despite the odds, you're going to win. I just know it. It's kind of like when I won the Mr. Eastbrooke contest."

I start laughing. "What are you even talking about? That was high school."

"Doesn't matter. I really wanted to win—not because I needed another trophy, but because I wanted to prove a point."

"And what point was that?"

I get the grin. The grin that grows into the megawatt, brighter-than-the-sunset smile.

The sunlight is hitting his strong, stubble-covered jawline. I slide my hands up onto broad shoulders that still taper down to a lean torso. And my eyes fall on the little freckle on his cheek. Just like it did on the day I'm pretending not to remember. The day he took my advice and risked making a fool of himself in front of the whole school just to show me that he loved me.

"You know exactly what it was. That the only people you should care what they think are the people you love. And the people you love want you to win. What do you say? Do we have a bet?"

"Sure. Why not?" I say, giving him a steamy kiss.

NEWS FLASH

Live update from the Oscars Watch Party!

I'm not usually one to brag, but if you aren't following me on social media, you totally should be.

BECAUSE I AM AT THE CAPTIVE FILMS OSCARS WATCH PAR-TAY!

#sorrynotsorry

The crew from the movie is here, minus the ones up for awards, but, people, Tommy Stevens, Abby Johnston, and their adorable preteen son, Lincoln, just walked in. Can I just say, this couple embodies my life goals? They look so happy and in love, and Abby looks like she is still thirty. I don't know how she does it.

If you watched The Keatyn Chronicles movies, you will be a big fan of Keatyn's Grandpa Douglas. I heard that he continues to invest in Captive Films, and he is also here with his lovely wife of more than fifty years. #swoon

OVER THE COURSE of the evening, I am able to interview Abby, who is totally gracious and forthcoming, but she would not give up the details on what designer Keatyn might be wearing tonight. She *swore*, she didn't know.

Something I didn't know that she went on to tell me is that while, sometimes, celebrities collaborate with a designer to create a custom gown, other times, their stylist just wheels in a rack of dresses, and they decide right before they go. She told me that one time she switched gowns at the last minute because a jeweler offered to let her wear the most beautiful emerald necklace she'd ever seen, and the pink frock she'd planned on wearing didn't go. Instead, she decided on a beautiful black Valentino ballgown. That may have been when I screamed and nearly peed my pants.

Because don't you remember sitting on your couch at home, watching the Awards, when Abby stepped onto the red carpet in that dress, looking like a million bucks? Actually, it was about 2.9 million bucks, based on the value of the jewels.

The excitement here continues when Avery Stevens, the oldest of the triplets, shows up with a very handsome young man on her arm. I had not a clue who he was and even resorted to snapping a stealth photo of him and then doing an image search. When that didn't work, I grabbed another champagne bottle off one of the tables and filled up their glasses. What I learn is that her adorable escort's name is Kyle and that he works at the vineyard in event planning. They declined to comment on their relationship, but I can tell you that their relationship includes a lot of sweet kissing.

Ah, to be young again.

The next big entrances are the other two triplets, Ivery and Emery, sans dates but with their full girl squad. All looked fabulous and perfect in their short little skirts and skimpy club-like outfits and took many selfies.

Just when I thought I was looking hot, some nineteen-year-olds have to show up and ruin everything.

Gracie Stevens, who I ask if she gave her sister advice on what to do when you are nominated, simply shrugs, wraps her arm around her hot date, Summer Boy, Dylan, and escorts him over to their family table, grabbing a few glasses of champagne on the way.

LIVE ON THE RED CARPET has been airing on the big screen with the sound turned off in lieu of festive music. I about drop my plate of appetizers when it switches over, and a loud voice announces that Keatyn has arrived.

And holy shit. She's always looked red-carpet worthy every time she steps outside. Constantly in the spotlight since she was only eighteen, she's never made a bad fashion move. Her style—what I like to call edgy princess—always includes soft, luscious pastels or sparkly golds. Even when she was starring in the *Trinity* movies, playing a kick-ass heroine, she never wore black to an event.

So when she steps out of the limo in black from head to toe, my mouth gapes open.

A reporter immediately shoves a microphone in her face. "Keatyn, congratulations on your nomination. Tell us about your gown."

"A Kym and Gellen original. Jewels, Harry Winston. Shoes, Gucci."

"Uh, thanks," the reporter says, clearly still in shock, too. She doesn't even ask her anything else.

Keatyn looks gorgeous. But different. Her eyes are smoky, her skin flawless. Her hair is pulled back into a tight, high ponytail, held in place by a band of rhinestones with black feathers hanging down from skinny leather threads—an accessory that is sure to spark a trend.

The necklace wrapped around her neck is slightly asymmetrical, one side gleaming in a black metal and the other forming a feather of black diamonds. Her dress is black, strapless, and fluid but shimmers from every angle. Bondage-like leather straps wrap around her waist and hips, highlighting her curves. Her shoes are black and caged.

She looks … fierce.

And like a freaking winner.

I'm calling it now. Best Dressed—is Keatyn Arrington!

THE DOLBY THEATER – HOLLYWOOD

Keatyn

THE BEST ACTRESS in a Leading Role is the next award to be announced. I sit up straight in my seat and smile, knowing the cameras will be moving back and forth between us as we watch a video montage of the nominees. The scenes are poignant and heartwarming. And I really do feel thrilled just to be nominated.

This film is special to me in many ways—the fact that it was a big risk for Captive, that it was as much a labor of love as being pregnant, and that it was something completely out of the box for both me and Knox. I've never lacked for motivation when filming. I always easily slide in and out of my roles, but this one was … more important, I guess. Not just because so much was riding on it, but also because, for the first time, I allowed it to get personal. To allow my relationship with Aiden to guide me. To pretend it was him I was looking at and not Knox.

Aiden takes my hand in his, like he's reading my mind and he knows what I'm thinking. I give it a squeeze back because he's the reason I was nominated. He's the reason I was able to portray a woman who loved the same soul throughout time—because she fully believed in true love, fate, and destiny.

He leans over and gives me a sweet kiss on the cheek as the announcer says, "The envelope, please."

Dramatic pause.

"And the Oscar goes to … Keatyn Arrington."

Knox leaps out of his chair, pulling me up with him, jumping up and down, and hugging me. Riley and Dallas join in the fray, and Knox practically has to push me toward the stage. I'm pretty sure I'm in shock. I look back at Aiden, who rubs his fingers together, signaling that he won his bet and I need to pay up.

When I get up onstage, an award is thrust into my hand. I'm given hugs by the presenters, and then I'm left alone in front of the microphone.

It's then that I realize I'm supposed to say something. Aiden was right. I should have prepared a speech just in case.

"I'm sorry, everyone. I didn't write a speech because I never in a million years thought I'd be standing up here," I confess. "In the industry, Knox and I were labeled as box office gold, but no matter how many fans lined up to see our movies, the critics never considered us *serious* actors. And, as I stand here in shock, I realize that I started to believe them.

"I'd like to thank the Academy. And Knox Daniels, who, when he first let me read his script, told me that it was the kind of story that would win awards. I need to thank Riley and Dawson Johnson, Dallas McMahon, and Grandpa Douglas, my partners at Captive Films, and the whole Captive family.

"And to our fans. You all know I'm a sucker for a good love story. Thank you for proving to me that critical and commercial success don't have to be mutually exclusive."

I find Aiden's beautiful green eyes in the crowd and feel like time stands still. I could be at Eastbrooke, kicking a goal at his face; at the top of the Eiffel Tower, saying, *I will*; at an altar, saying, *I do*; holding our new babies and saying, *We will*; or sitting in a rocking chair, hoping we can.

"And to Aiden. Thank you for being the control in my chaos. This is for you. Always. Only. Ever for you."

The music starts playing, and I'm escorted off the stage where I'm given a glass of champagne and told I will be escorted down the Winners Walk. But I won't do either.

Not yet.

I set the glass back on the tray. "Can you hold this for me until after Knox wins?"

"Of course," my escort says with a sweet smile.

Love Struck and Captive Films have had a surprisingly good run—winning Best Costume Design, Best Director, Best Original Screenplay, Best Original Song, and Best Picture besides my award. Now, it's time to find out if we really will beat the odds and sweep the Oscars.

Jennifer Edwards and a fellow actor walk out from stage left, opposite where I am, and take their place at the podium. They introduce each Best Actor in a Leading Role nominee, which seems to take forever.

I nervously tap my toe.

Finally, the envelope is handed to Jennifer.

As she rips the envelope open, her fellow actor says dramatically, "And the Oscar goes to …"

"Knox fucking Daniels!" Jennifer yells out and throws a fist pump into the air as she jumps up and down and cheers. "Whoop! Whoop!"

I realize I was holding my breath. I let it out as Katie leans over and whispers in Knox's ear before he stands up to take the stage.

When he gets there, Jennifer gives him a sloppy kiss on the side of his face and hands him the award. Much like I did, Knox stands in front of the microphone for a few moments. But it isn't out of shock. It's because he's choked up.

It makes me start to cry, and the crowd claps loudly, giving him a standing ovation.

"Thank you, everyone," he says, composing himself. "Sorry, I had a speech planned. I was going to thank a bunch of people, none of whose names I can remember right now." He shakes his head. "Did y'all see my beautiful wife kiss me and whisper something into my ear when they called my name? Yeah, well, she just told me she's pregnant. I'm not sure which I'm more shocked about."

The crowd goes nuts.

"Ohmigod!" I say out loud.

"Shit," Knox says, frowning. "Sorry, Katie, you probably didn't intend for me to just announce that to the millions watching." He does a fist pump into the air. "But fuck yeah! I'm going to be a dad!" Tears start to fill his eyes as he shakes his head in disbelief, looking at the award and then at Katie. "This might be the pinnacle of my career, but marrying you, sugar, is the greatest achievement of my life."

The music starts playing, indicating that his time is over, but Knox is just getting started.

His joy is palpable as he throws his arms up in the air and yells out, "I love you! I know the music is playing, but I gotta keep going." He looks offstage to where I'm standing. "Keatyn, damn. Has this been a long time coming or what? Riley Johnson, where are you, man? I love you! Dallas McMahon, buddy, love you! Dawson! I love you, man! Oh, shit, I can't forget Missy! Missy, you are the best assistant ever. And Miss Bossy Pants, Vanessa. You are the bombest PR we could ever ask for. Damian, man, for the beautiful song! And, Mom, oh, Mom! I know you're watching!" He taps his heart. "I love you!"

He looks up at the ceiling, his words catching in his throat. "And to my late dad. I just want you to know that I do believe in the beauty of my dreams.

"Thank you to the Academy. Thanks to the fans who went and saw the movie. Hell, thanks to everyone!"

He holds the trophy over his head and then is escorted offstage as the host goes back out to end the telecast.

When Knox sees that I waited for him, he pulls me into a hug. Then we share a tender moment, our foreheads touching, both of us crying.

Knox has been one of my best friends for over ten years. Our stars hitched upon each other's because of a crazy screen test that acting teachers now show as an example of what not to do.

"Whose dick did you suck to win that thing?" I whisper in his ear, using the exact same words he said to me when we first met and he was pissed they'd called him in to do a screen test with *a nobody*.

His head drops onto my shoulder as he bursts out laughing. "I was an asshole, wasn't I?"

"I'm pretty sure we were well matched in confidence levels," I reply. "Can you believe we're standing here? That we swept the fucking Academy Awards?"

"Hell yeah, I can believe it. I told you that script was going to win awards. Your speech was beautiful for something that wasn't planned."

"I had no idea I was going to win."

"That's because I didn't tell you that I wished on the moon for all of this," he teases.

"Very funny." I can't help but laugh. "And you're going to be a dad!"

"Now, that *did* fucking surprise me."

"Are you ready for your champagne now, Keatyn?" the steward asks, this time appearing with two flutes.

"I thought it was a tradition that, after you won, they gave you a glass, and you drank it before you went to your interviews?"

The steward laughs. "She said she wasn't going to drink without you."

Knox nods, his eyes getting misty.

I hold up my glass to him and whisper, "Here's to us. And, while you are stuck at home, pampering your pregnant wife, you need to write another freaking script."

NEWS FLASH

Live update from the Oscars Watch Party!

Okay, tears are streaming down my face.

A stunned Keatyn took the stage and gave an eloquent speech, one that should motivate future actors for decades to come.

Knox won.

Love Struck has swept the Oscars.

And, yes, it's wonderful that his former-schoolteacher wife is pregnant—*sob!*—but that's not what's made me completely lose my shit and start ugly crying.

It's the photo that just flashed on the screen.

Taken backstage.

Of Knox and Keatyn embracing. Their foreheads touching. Both overcome with emotion. About what they've accomplished together.

And for those of us—and by *us*, I mean, me—who have been following this pair since day one, it doesn't get any better than this. It's the pinnacle of all our careers.

Bottles are popping left and right, and I need to get in on that shit, so I'm signing off.

I have also been flirting with a very handsome man who tells me that he is a gaffer. I have no idea what that means, but I am *more* than willing to find out.

Happy Oscars, everyone! And congrats to the cast and crew of *Love Struck*! Here's to hoping this gaffer gets *love struck* by me tonight! I *am* wearing the lightning bolt pin that was handed out at the door.

THE DOLBY THEATER - HOLLYWOOD

Keatyn

WE'RE ESCORTED DOWN what is known as the Winners Walk. It takes us out the back of the theater and into a nearby hotel.

The first stop is the photo room where we pose with our trophies. And although, normally, this is something you do as individuals, we break the rules and stay together despite what we're told.

Next, we are escorted to the interview room where three hundred journalists with numbered paddles raise theirs in the hopes that we will answer their question. We stay until no one has any more questions. And, somewhere along the way, someone brought us shots.

Eventually, we get to the Governors Ball where Knox and I get our nameplates screwed on to our awards.

We make our appearances but very quickly head to the Captive Films party. Ariela and Vanessa worked long hours, setting up the viewing party for our employees, movie cast, movie crew, and all their families. And they invited all our movie industry friends.

But it's clear, when we get there, the celebration has been going on without us. We say a few words, pass around our shiny trophies, toast each other, then Aiden pulls me out to the dance floor.

He's beaming, and I know why. He won our bet.

"What's the smile for?" I ask him. "You thrilled for everyone at Captive?"

"No, I'm thrilled for us."

"You tricked me, I think. Into this whole fourth-baby thing."

"Nah," he says, sliding his hand up my back. "You didn't think you'd win. I gotta be honest; I wanted you to win more than anything, and I thought you deserved it, but you convinced me that you wouldn't. I was just screwing around, using it as a way to delicately broach the subject." He lowers his head and nips at my neck in the most delicious way. "If you ask me, it was sorta like fate."

I smile, knowing he's probably right.

Fate definitely played a role in our path to love, although I did my best to fight it. I remember, at one point, when I was a teen, saying that I wanted to kick fate's ass. I am pretty sure I even Googled how to do it. And, although much of what has happened in our life has been due to hard work, a supportive family, and a whole lot of love, I can't deny that fate has seemed to play a role.

And I have been thinking about another baby. After all, my mom and Tommy had triplets and then had my little sister, Gracie, and I can't imagine a life without her.

"I disagree, Aiden. I don't think it was sorta like fate. I think it was exactly like fate," I reply.

He increases the pressure of his lips, letting them stroll down my neck.

"Would my award winner want to go home and allow me to collect on our bet?"

"Hmm, not yet. We have too much celebrating left to do, but … I'm not opposed to a quick trip out to the limo."

He looks up at me, his green eyes shining with desire, then leads me off the dance floor.

SATURDAY, MARCH 5TH
ASHER VINEYARDS – SONOMA COUNTY

Riley

"I DO—AGAIN," DALLAS says, kissing his bride, RiAnne, under a rustic arch covered in brightly colored flowers.

"I now pronounce you husband and wife ... again."

"Woo-hoo!" everyone yells out as Dallas and RiAnne make their way down the aisle, their five children in tow.

THE SOUNDS OF happiness fill the air—kids screaming with delight, friends engaged in warm conversations, wine glasses clinking, and laughter. Lots and lots of laughter.

I look around at the organized chaos that is Dallas and RiAnne's vow renewal.

"It turned out beautifully, don't you think?" Ariela asks as she hands me a glass of a rich red cabernet.

"You turned out beautifully," I tell her, letting my eyes wander down the silky fabric flowing fluidly across her body. I touch my finger to her shoulder, sliding it across her delicate collarbone.

She smiles at me and swats my hand away, so I take the opportunity to glide it across her ass instead.

"Riley, behave."

"Since when have I ever behaved?" I flirt.

She rolls her eyes and pulls me into a hot kiss. "Pretty much never. I was asking what you thought of the venue, not my dress. You know, the project I've been working on for the last year and a half."

"Oh, that. Hard to notice details like brick-lined paths, floral arches, lantern-lined terraces, and rustic-chic pavilions when you're wearing a dress like that."

"What about the bounce houses, Ferris wheel, and the lawn games for all the kids?"

"They are awesome." I wipe the smile off my face, stop flirting, and say seriously, "All joking aside, Ariela, the facility is amazing. Kyle told me that it's booked up for the next year."

She looks into my eyes. "When I came to California to find you, I ended up finding so much more."

"What'd you find, kitty?"

"Me. And the life I always dreamed about."

"You mean, we always dreamed about," I tease.

"Yes, in fact, I think it was you, during your best-man toast, who said that, when you surround yourself with the people you love, great things can happen. I think that's the story of your life, Riley Johnson."

I wrap my arm around her shoulders as we both look out at the people we love, all laughing, dancing, drinking, and carrying on. I make eye contact with Aiden from across the room. He gives me a subtle nod, letting me know that everything is ready.

"What do you say we go take a walk? It's dark now, and they're all dancing. No one will notice we're gone. Besides, I have something to show you."

"What?" she says, slipping her hand into mine.

"Well, while you've been working on your masterpiece here, Aiden and I have been working on something on my land."

"Oh, I am well aware of the project that must not be named." She giggles. "Are you ever going to tell me what's going on back there? And, more importantly, are we going to be able to take down the awful construction plastic covering it before your parents come out to see the completed guesthouses?"

I lead her to a Gator and then wrap a blanket around her shoulders to keep her warm during the ride.

"Actually, yes," I tell her. "It seems the stars have aligned, and your project is done at the same time mine is. So, yes, when the whole family descends on the West Coast for Easter, everything will be ready."

We drive down one of the paths that we installed over the last year and a half that connects the vineyard to Knox's property and the studio and then on down to our house. We finished the renovations of the inside of the house about six months ago, and I love it so much that I sold my penthouse. With the guesthouses nearly finished, it means that my dreams are also nearly complete.

Almost.

There's something I have to do tonight.

As we pull around our house, she notices it.

"What are all those lights in our backyard, Riley? It looks like a Friday night football game. What's going on?"

"You'll see," I say, laying my hand on her knee and giving it a little squeeze.

"Riley Johnson, did you put in a field just so your family could play touch football at Thanksgiving?"

I grin. "Maybe."

"Wow," she says as we come down the hill and she can see the full view. "Ohmigod! You even painted the end zones with your name! And it's all decorated in our high school colors!"

I grab a set of red and yellow pom-poms out of the back of the cart and toss them at her.

"Are you kidding me? Pom-poms, too?"

"Well, if I'm going to play on this field, I hope you'd still want to cheer for me. You know how those little skirts used to turn me on."

She swats me with one of the poms as I lead her to the center of the field. "That, I do remember. Do you remember when you first asked me to be your girlfriend? You dragged me out of the cheer line, put that four-leaf clover tattoo on my face, and asked me to be your lucky charm." She slides her arms around my waist, much like she did on that night. "And then you told me that you loved me for the first time. You never did anything small."

I laugh along with her. "Well, I am a Johnson."

"Speaking of Johnsons," she says, looking down.

I point toward my junk. "This one?"

She laughs again in the shy way she did when we first met. When I believed that we would be together forever from that moment on. Life didn't go exactly the way I'd planned, but at this point, it doesn't matter because I'm here with her. Right now.

She points down at the monogram in the middle of the field. "I get why you have your last name in the end zones, but why do you have an *A* in the middle of the field? Is Asher Vineyards going to borrow it sometimes or something?"

"No, the *A* is for you, Ariela. Because you and I are back here, starting a new life together. A new chapter to our epic love story."

"It's funny," she says. "Keatyn and I were talking about that the other day. About how it's not where you've been that matters; it's where you end up that does."

"That's right. We've ended up here. And I finally understand what the hell that saying even means. So here goes. Ariela, I've been directing movies and videos for over ten years, which means I understand the difference between a happy ending and a happily ever after."

"And does one of those involve a blow job?" she says with a laugh.

I laugh and shake my head. "No. If this were the movie of our life, this would be our happy ending. We're back together where we belong. I could end it here with a kiss under some twinkle lights, and the audience would be happy."

"Kiss me then, Riley. Give me my happy ending," she says with an adorable grin.

"Says the girl who made me wait fifty-four days for sex and about killed me."

"You remember that?"

"I remember you were the only girl ever worth the wait."

She smiles at me with tears in her eyes. I grab her hand and tightly pull it to my chest.

"Ariela, I'd rather not end our movie here."

"Why not? Everything is perfect."

"Because a happy ending isn't good enough for our movie."

"It's not?" she asks, looking slightly confused.

But then the stadium lights are turned off, and the strands of twinkle lights that stretch from end zone to end zone are turned on as a band starts playing our song.

"What is all this, Riley?" she asks, looking around in awe.

"What this is, Ariela, my dear, is what I hope is the start of our happily ever after." I take her hand back in mine and then drop to one knee. "Since you came back into my life, everything has meaning. Suddenly, I care about everything. Because you are my everything—my all-encompassing,   still-can-hardly-breathe-when-you're-around everything. Will you marry me, have babies with me, and love me forever?"

The second I stand up, she jumps into my arms. If I didn't have damn good balance, I would be flat on my ass right now. I grab her tiny waist and lean her back just a little.

Just enough to give her a happily ever after–worthy kiss.

"You didn't even let me show you the ring before you said yes," I tease her.

She holds up her hand, showing me the Hello Kitty ring I gave her on that football field so many years ago. Back then, I loved her, but all I could think about was getting myself under that cute little cheerleading skirt. Now, I want so much more than that—a bunch of screaming kids and my own mansion of love.

I'm shaky when I pull the ring box out of my pocket. I'm nervous about this part.

Although her body language is definitely saying yes, she's still yet to actually answer my question. I open the box and show her the large pink diamond ring I had custom-designed.

She freezes, her body tensing up, and I'm afraid she hates it. But

Aiden told me not to freak out if she cries. He said that crying is good in this situation. *But what if she says no?*

Tears stream down her face. "It's pink. Like the sparkly ring you gave me when you asked me out. But a little more grown-up."

She throws her arms around me and kisses me.

"Yes, Riley! Yes! I can't wait to start my happily ever after with you."

And, when the band has stopped playing and the twinkle lights are turned off, I lie under the stars and make love to the only girl I've ever really loved, who will *always* hold my heart captive.

About the Author

Jillian is a *USA TODAY* bestselling author who writes fun romances with characters her readers fall in love with, from the boy next door in the *That Boy* trilogy to the daughter of a famous actress in *The Keatyn Chronicles* to a kick-ass young assassin in the *Spy Girl* series.

She lives in a small Florida beach town, is married to her college sweetheart, has two grown children, and two Labrador Retrievers named Cali and Camber. When she's not working, she likes to travel, paint, shop for shoes, watch football, and go to the beach.

Check out Jillian's website at www.jilliandodd.net for added content and to sign up for her newsletter.

Made in the USA
Middletown, DE
14 November 2018